D1555938

The Earl's Defiant Wallflower

ERICA RIDLEY

Four left for war...

Only three made it home.

Chapter One

January 1816
London, England

It could be worse, Lord Oliver York reminded himself as he trained his narrowed eyes on this newest battlefield. It had been three years since he'd set foot in a ballroom. The styles had changed and the faces had aged, but London soirées were as treacherous as ever. He tried to relax. At least no one was shooting at him.

When he'd left home, he'd been plain Mr. Oliver York, heir apparent to a silent dictator whom he'd been certain would live forever. Full of ennui and patriotism, he'd defied his father and skipped off to fight the French with his three best friends. Because, what was the worst that could happen?

Answer: War.

He'd lost all three of his best friends. Edmund had been felled by an enemy rifle. Xavier hadn't spoken a word in months. And Bartholomew... Oliver had lost that friend when he'd had the bad grace to save the man's life.

Not that Oliver could blame him. Bart had made it back to England without his left leg or his brother. He would rather have died than let go of his dying twin. He would have succeeded in that endeavor, had Oliver not hefted his mangled body in his arms and speared his way through the bloody battlefield to the last surviving sawbones.

It was a miracle the man survived. An even bigger miracle that he hadn't picked up the first blade he'd chanced upon and driven it between Oliver's ribs.

Heroes, all of them. Heroes and murderers.

They each had blood on their hands. Scars in their hearts. One couldn't slice a bayonet through someone's neck to save one's own, and then pick right back up in London with carriage races and drunken wagers.

Drunken, yes. He was very good at drunken. Alcohol was the only thing that dulled the anger. And the guilt.

There had been no postal service on the front lines, so he'd actually made it all the way to his front door before the rest of the news had reached him.

He'd lost his father. Oliver was earl now. *Congratulations.*

His father—per the subsequent scandal sheets—had come to his untimely end in the bed of his latest mistress, when her cook, unaware of his seafood allergy, had sent a tray of salad tossed with lime and prawn to the lovers' boudoir.

Death by salad. And just like that, Oliver inherited an earldom.

He didn't know a button about being earl, of course. His father had rarely even spoken to him; therefore Oliver was in no position to replace him. It would take months just to go through the journals and correspondence.

Nor was he in the market for a wife. He could scarcely be responsible for one. He was having a hard enough time wrangling this beast of an earldom without adding a dependent to the mix. Not with his future uncertain, his past a nightmare.

Men of his class didn't marry for love. Men with his past shouldn't marry at all.

War had taught him that there was no vulnerability like being helpless to save someone he cared about. Like his best friends.

Xavier still had a chance to recover. At the moment, he was propped up in the library like a great silent doll, but Oliver had faith his listless friend would come out of his fugue.

That belief was precisely why Oliver, savior of all people who did not wish to be saved, had shoved his friend into a carriage and forced them both into an environment alive with lights and color. He might be dead inside, but he refused to allow the same to happen to Xavier.

Captain Xavier Grey had once been the jolliest rattle of them all. Now, he was one ragged breath away from catatonia.

Surgeons were at a loss. He was more dead than alive, but there was nothing visibly wrong with him. Perhaps all he needed was some re-assimilation. Wine. Women. Dancing. A reminder of what they'd fought for, and what was still worth living for.

So Oliver had sent for his friend and an army of tailors. The two of them could out-dandy Brummel himself. Xavier had been easy enough to shepherd along, since he was mute and pliant as waxwork. Perhaps a smidgen more lifeless.

And now they were at a ball. One look at Oliver's face ensured no one would deny them entrance. But what was he to do with Xavier? He had fallen off his chair when Oliver had attempted to seat him in the ballroom with the spinsters, so Oliver had been forced to settle him in the library, in a wingback chair with plenty of pillows.

That had worked. Somewhat. The man hadn't changed position in the past two hours, and would likely sit there like a lump of clay right through Armageddon.

Oliver trudged from the library back to the ballroom. He clearly wasn't curing Xavier tonight. Maybe the one most in need of wine, women, and dancing was Oliver himself.

Except the ratafia was warm, the wine bitter, the music off-pace. The debutantes were only attracted to his ignominiously gained title. The men only approached him to hear gore-splattered war stories Oliver had no inclination to retell, much less relive.

Ballroom Waterloo. The deafening orchestra, the cloying perfume, the swirls of satin and lace—it was as much a hell as the battlefield he'd escaped.

Anybody who fantasized about war was an imbecile. Anyone who fantasized about inheriting a title was an even bigger imbecile. This whole ballroom was chock full of imbeciles, and Oliver was the biggest of them all for thinking Xavier was a soldier he could save, this soirée a skirmish he could win. He didn't know these people anymore. He wasn't certain he even wished to. He curled his hands into fists.

Look at them planning their attacks. Sharpening their rapier wits. All of them, pawns in the same war, playing the parts they were born to play. He could no more have escaped inheriting his earldom than a wallflower could avoid being labeled a—

Oliver frowned. Brow furrowed, he squinted through the swirl of dancing couples and frowned again.

There was a girl. Across the room. Pressed into the wallpaper. A pretty girl who didn't know her part.

Not a wallflower, this young woman, despite her back-to-the-wall stance. True wallflowers dressed in drab colors and did their best to blend with the shadows. This one wore a gown with enough silk and lace to befit an empress. The colors could blind a peacock. Her cleavage would tempt the Prince of Wales himself.

And yet, something about her gave the impression that her come-hither bodice and opulent trappings were nothing more than costuming. The true her—whoever that might be—was hidden from the naked eye. Oliver narrowed his own. Something in the set of her jaw, the stiffness in her spine, the softness of those ripe, full lips...

Even as he watched, she trapped her plump lower lip beneath a row of straight white teeth. Dark hair. Pale skin. Voluptuous curves. He shifted his weight.

This Snow White belonged to a different type of bedtime story. What man wouldn't want those soft red lips on every part of his body? She must've infatuated half of London by now. The virginal lace at her bosom, the way those thick black lashes blinked a few more times than strictly necessary...

Oliver's intrigued half-smile died on his face as he realized the truth. This wasn't coquetry. His enticing wallflower was uncomfortable. Nervous. His fingers curled into fists. Where the devil was her chaperone? Her friends? Hell, her suitors? She was utterly alone.

Someone this beautiful, with skin that fair and hair that dark couldn't have any difficulty attracting a man.

"Got your eye on the new one, Carlisle?" came a sly whisper from behind Oliver's shoulder. "Better dip your wick now, before all the others have their way. Miss Macaroni won't be looking half as nubile once she's had a mouthful of—"

"Macaroni?" Oliver interrupted, barely managing to tamp down his impulse to plug his fist into the speaker's face, sight unseen. He wouldn't be able to resist the temptation for long. War did that to a man.

The voice chuckled. "Eh, she's a Yank. Best thing for anyone to do is keep a hand over her mouth, because you can't understand a single word coming out of it."

Oh, mother-loving shite. That was Phineas Mapleton talking. The *ton's* worst gossip.

"Not that anyone'd want her for conversation anyway," Mapleton continued. "Every female worth her salt has already given her the cut direct. The only creatures putting themselves in her path now are the desperate hostesses and the profligates planning to give her a tumble or two. Dirty money, dirty gel. Not much else a chit like that can hope for. Old man Jarvis already put his name down in White's as being the first to tup her. Got fifty quid on it, myself. Want to add your name to the pot?"

His lip curled in disgust. Ballrooms were treacherous indeed. This jackanapes had an innocent American in his sights. One who didn't even seem to have a duenna, much less friends to keep away wolves like Mapleton.

Oliver's temple began to throb as he forced his fists to unclench. This was a different type of combat, he reminded himself. The worst thing to do would be to make a scene with Mapleton. The scandal would be horrific.

Yet he couldn't walk away. Not when the wallflower needed *rescuing*. His goddamn Achilles' heel, no matter how disastrous the outcome tended to be. He wished his heroics would work out for once.

He kept his eyes trained on the pretty black-haired American, every muscle tensed for action. An eternity ticked by. No one approached her. She had no one to dance with, to talk to. She looked... lost. Hauntingly lonely. Frightened and defiant all at the same time.

'Twould be better for them both if he turned around right now. Never met her eye. Never exchanged a single word. Left her to her fate and him to his.

It was already too late.

Chapter Two

The plan had seemed so simple when Grace Halton's mother had first proposed it. Sail from Pennsylvania to England, meet her long-lost grandparents, and use their modest dowry to attract a husband capable and willing to provide for both Grace and her ailing mother.

Three simple steps. Three exercises in futility and failure.

First catastrophe: the ocean. Grace had spent the entire transatlantic journey with her face in her chamber pot, more than willing to trade the endless waves and deadening horizon for the flimsy, landlocked shack she'd shared with her mother.

Second disaster: her grandparents. They'd been aghast at Grace's uncanny resemblance to their black-haired, green-eyed daughter. Almost every word out of their mouths since had been a criticism of Grace's bearing or person or upbringing or education. Or reiterating that her dowry money hinged upon her finding the groom of whom they approved.

All of which made step three—Operation Husband—that much more difficult. She didn't just need a beau. Attracting a suitor was a brainless, simple goal every debutante in this ballroom expected to accomplish by the end of the Season.

Grace didn't have that long. Not with her mother so sick. She needed someone who could be brought to scratch—and to the altar—in a matter of days.

But the invitations her grandparents' money attracted weren't for venues like Almack's. These were smaller soirées, in private homes. The "Marriage Mart" was quite out of Grace's reach. What she had were a handful of hostesses for whom the novelty of an American guest was worth an invitation to dinner. If she made a good impression on the right people, there might be more invitations to occasional dinner parties in her future.

But she didn't have a future. She had right now. And time was running out.

Grace shook off her despondency and straightened her spine. There was only one path forward. She needed a wealthy, controllable, kindhearted, grandparent-approved, banns-read-and-bells-rung *husband*, and she needed him Right. Now. If she didn't return in the next few weeks with enough coin to save her mother and their home, there wouldn't be a mother or a home to come back to.

It seemed insurmountable. If a gentleman was remotely moneyed and kindhearted and marriage-minded, he'd been snapped up long before Grace's spindly legs had trembled ashore.

Her accent had taken care of the rest.

She'd set sail believing in her mother's bedtime tales of glittering ballrooms and bejeweled gowns befitting a princess, promising Grace she'd be likely to have the *ton* at her feet and her hand on the altar before the first week was through.

But the only Brits willing to look down their noses long enough to speak to her were the fops so desperate for attention that even a gauche American would suffice, or the decrepit old libertines so entranced by pretty young flesh that they didn't much care what her accent sounded like. After all, they didn't plan to *speak* with her.

Even the lady's maid her grandparents kept sending along as a chaperone consistently disappeared within seconds of arrival. If a paid servant had better things to do than be seen publicly in Grace's orbit, what hope was there for finding a husband?

At this point, what she mostly could use was a friend. But even *that* was hopeless.

The most exalted of the English roses would have naught to do with her. Grace was not only a penniless American; her grandparents' small dowry carried the filthy taint of *trade*. And worse.

Grace's grandfather had invested in some sort of fabric processing plant during the American Revolution, and then purchased a handful of sword and bayonet armament factories just as Napoleon rose to power. The recent battle of Waterloo had put paid to Napoleon's rule, but Grace's grandparents had become rich off the spilled blood of their countrymen. She shivered at the thought. No wonder she was a pariah.

"Cold, *chérie*?" A rich but toothless roué grinned down at her over the curve of his gold-plated cane, marriage—or rather, the marriage bed—obviously on his mind. "A turn with me in one of the balconies might warm those bare shoulders, eh?"

Grace leaped to her feet and out from under his calculated gaze. She'd thought herself invisible among the sea of spinsters and chaperones along the far wall, but the come-hither cut of her fashion-plate gown had undoubtedly given her away. Three weeks of seasickness had whittled the plumpness from her body, giving her a wasp waist and actual cheekbones for the first time in her life.

Such a diet was not one Grace could recommend. Especially since it seemed to go hand in glove with attracting the lecherous eye of men older than her grandfather.

"Sorry," she blurted in a tone that indicated she was anything but. "This set is already promised."

She all but flew out of his palsied grasp, sidestepping the matrons to squeeze against the shadowed wainscoting at the opposite end of the ballroom.

This corner was too close to the orchestra to hear oneself think, too far from the food and drink to engender even idle conversation. The icy draft from a second-floor balcony kept away anyone whose blood was still circulating, and the wax spitting from the last taper in the chandelier overhead marked this square meter as uninhabitable.

She crossed her goose-pimpled arms over her ruched bodice, mindless of the thick moulding digging into the small of her back or the clumps of wax sticking to her silk slippers. Her gaze darted about the ballroom. Elegant couples began a lively country-dance. Grace hugged herself tighter. She had never felt less like dancing.

Not that she'd been asked.

Her jaw clenched. She hadn't any idea how to accomplish any of her goals. Without her grandparents' money, she couldn't return to her homeland. Without a husband, she couldn't get her grandparents' money. Without a noble birth and a British accent, she couldn't attract a man interested in something other than her dowry or her virginity. She ground her teeth.

Back home in Pennsylvania, she'd had friends of both sexes, who loved her for herself and not for something they might take from her. Back home in Pennsylvania, they would've had a right belly laugh to see Gracie Halton trussed up in finery and mincing about a suffocating ballroom. Back home in Pennsylvania, her mother— her mother—

Grace's breath caught and her eyes blurred. Oh, who *knew* what was going on back home in Pennsylvania? She'd written her mother and her neighbors every day since she'd stepped off the boat, and had yet to receive a single word of response.

Fear gripped her. Was her mother still in the threadbare bed Grace had last seen her in? Was she even still alive? Was there still time? Or had Grace flung herself headlong into a fool's mission that only ensured she would not be present in her mother's last hours, when she needed her daughter most?

Blindly, Grace pushed away from the velvet-lined wall...

Right into the path of a giant as tall and as hard as an oak.

A firm hand caught her about the waist as strong fingers captured her wrists. She blinked the sting of unshed tears from her eyes to find herself entangled not with an oak, but with a man possessed of dark brown hair and dangerous golden brown eyes. A wry smile curved his lips as the orchestra began the opening strains of a waltz.

The hot muscles beneath her palms were hard and firm—no need for a tailor's touch to improve *this* sculpted body. He was impossibly tall and uncomfortably close. But unlike the other trussed turkeys sweltering inside the breezeless room, his clothes didn't reek of day-old perfume. His eyes weren't bloodshot or blasé, but rather clear and warm and drinking her in as if he were two seconds away from yanking her close enough to claim her mouth. Her heart thundered.

Everything about him was raw heat and restrained power. The exact opposite of what she was looking for. If a man like this took a wife, he would never let her slip away.

She forced her starving lungs to breathe. She was making a cake of herself. She'd almost mown down this exquisite hulk of a man, like the unsophisticated American they all believed her to be. He was simply protecting the herd by putting himself in the path of the rampaging bull.

Heat flooded her cheeks as she broke eye contact. She'd never felt so foolish and uncultured in her life.

Her breath hitched, but she forced herself to meet his eyes. A warm, honey brown. Someone this gorgeous definitely had somewhere better to be. She tugged at her wrists, signaling he was free to go. Only a fool would try to keep him.

He dropped one of his hands, but did not immediately hurry away, as she had anticipated. He seemed even larger than before.

His free hand tightened at her waist. "Shall we dance?"

Just like that, her legs could barely hold her steady. She tilted into his touch, conscious that he must be able to feel her body tremble beneath his fingers. Why would he wish to dance with her? He was too young to be a roué, too gentlemanly to be a rake, too well-heeled to be desperate for money, too smolderingly attractive to be in want of female companionship.

But it couldn't hurt to make certain.

She narrowed her eyes and forced her mind back on her mission. She needed a husband with money. "Are your pockets to let?"

He blinked at her in confusion. "What? No!"

"Are you in the market for a wife?"

"*Hell* no!" His sculpted cheekbones flushed a subtle pink as he belatedly recalled he was speaking to a lady. "That is to say, at some point, it is my duty to take a wife."

"Close enough." Grace slid her wrist from his fingers and placed her hand in his. "This dance is yours."

Chapter Three

It wasn't until the dark-haired vixen was already in his arms that Oliver realized just how badly he'd bollocsed the rescue mission. He'd swept the incomparable wallflower into a waltz before all and sundry, and he didn't even know her name. His shoulders tensed. He certainly put the *err* in knight errant.

Perhaps in America, Yankees could twirl comely strangers about a ballroom, but here in England, proper decorum dictated that gentlemen not even address an unknown maiden until they had been properly introduced, lest he publicly embarrass them both.

Yet it was already done. The slender fingers of her right hand nestled in his left, and his right palm was pressed flush against the delicate silk covering her equally delicate back. Her lips were even more tempting now that they were close enough to taste. She smelled like honey and wildflowers. He tried not to notice.

"What's your name?" he whispered urgently. Soft black eyelashes framed captivatingly green eyes. He couldn't look away.

She lifted a brow. "What do the others call me?"

The arch look on her face indicated she already knew the answer. He grimaced. Certainly she could not expect him to repeat the horrible appellation aloud.

She stared back at him without blinking. The seconds ticked closer to minutes.

"Macaroni," he admitted.

"That'll be *Miss* Macaroni to you." Her eyes laughed up at him.

He pulled her a little closer. And realized that, whether she laughed or not, hearing those words on someone's lips had to hurt. His mouth tightened. He would not contribute to such rumors.

"We must pretend to already know each other," he explained as they twirled in time with the music.

She arched a slender black brow. "Why?"

He blinked. What did she mean, why? They were waltzing together without even having been presented. "For your reputation, of course."

"My reputation is a piece of pasta. What more could you need to know?"

"Smith? Jones?" he pled desperately. Did she not understand the peril to young ladies who broke proscribed rules? "Certainly you have some other name, unrelated to foodstuffs."

Her lips curved. "Since you're the first to inquire, I'll let you in on the secret. I am Miss Halton."

He smiled back at her. Miss Halton. He liked how it sounded on her lips.

Before he could share his own name, her eyes narrowed. "Why are you dancing with me?"

The practiced words floated from his lips without thinking. "Who wouldn't wish to dance with a young lady as beautiful as you?"

"Everyone," she answered flatly. "This is the first I've been asked since arriving in England." She lifted her lips closer to his ear. "The stink of trade keeps the smarter suitors away."

He choked behind the pointed edges of his cravat. "Who would say such a thing to you?"

She raised her brows. "Nobody. Absolutely no one speaks to me. I'm left to assume the stink of trade is self-evident."

He caught himself lowering his face closer to the shining black curls piled atop her head. Quickly, he straightened his spine afore any onlookers might notice the gaffe.

She noticed, of course. Her light green eyes twinkled.

"You smell of jasmine," he said, after clearing his throat. "It's quite a lovely scent."

"It's bath soap. I'll have to write a note of appreciation to the manufacturer."

So would he. He took another sniff. His pulse raced as he fought the urge to twirl her right out of the ballroom. Either the scent or the woman—or likely a combination of both—had infiltrated his brain with images he really ought not to be having about Miss Halton in nothing but warm water and a few jasmine-scented bubbles. His throat convulsed.

He needed to steer this conversation back to safety. Such as completing the bloody introductions. Unless she hadn't asked because his title had already preceded him?

"If you didn't know," he said, "I am the Earl of Carlisle."

"I... did... not," she replied. "How splendid for you."

"Is it? I much preferred being Mr. Oliver York," he found himself admitting. He nearly stumbled as his words sank in. Why on earth would he say something that heretical to a total stranger, when he wouldn't confess it to his best friends?

Perhaps because Miss Halton *was* a total stranger, he realized. An ostracized American who not only held little interest in English propriety, but also had an utter lack of ears to gossip to, should the inclination ever cross her mind.

"I should have preferred that as well," she said, much to his surprise. "Pity."

He blinked in shock. She might not care about British nobility, but there was nothing abhorrent about being an earl, for shite's sake. Before he could reply, her rosebud lips were once again parting.

"It could be worse. At least you're not out hunting dowries."

"How gratifying you've found something to recommend me," he said between closed teeth. Why was she even here, if she held such disdain for his compatriots?

"Oh, I wouldn't recommend you."

He stared at her twinkling eyes for a second and then found himself biting back a grin. Had she really just set him in his place? The corners of his mouth twitched. *He* seemed far more in need of rescuing than the sharp-tongued Miss Halton. Being titled certainly hadn't impressed her. For someone cast into the lot of social pariah for nothing more than an accident of geography, she seemed to delight in acting the role of termagant.

He was appalled to find it a bit… refreshing.

After escaping the dark cloud around his usual companions, it was a relief to converse with a disinterested third party. Someone who didn't want something he could never give. Someone who had never seen the ravages of war. Someone with whom he did not share a past.

Someone with knowing eyes and pouting lips and a slender waist.

He forced himself to loosen his grip. "What shall we say when people ask us how we met? It needs to be something respectable. And believable."

"There's nothing more believable than the truth. We'll simply say I was strolling about, minding my own business, when you appeared out of nowhere and dragged me bodily to the dance floor."

He nodded once. "I've a better idea. Let's make up something completely untruthful."

The corners of her mouth twitched. "Aha. We'll say I was in my nightrail, brushing my hair in peaceful solitude, when you climbed up to my balcony and—"

"Do you even have a balcony?"

She pursed her lips. "You're not invited upon it, regardless."

He gave her a slow, naughty smile. "No one's ever *invited* to scale a balcony."

"Some women might be convinced to let you try." Her teasing gaze heated his skin.

"Let's start over," he suggested, rather than consider what the fictional Oliver might do after climbing up her balcony. Answer: everything.

"Why?" Her lips quirked. "Are we not having fun?"

"We're having far too much fun."

"These parties are *supposed* to be boring?" She lifted an eyebrow.

He gave her a stern nod, well aware his eyes betrayed his humor. "Precisely. You're meant to remark upon the weather, and I upon... the tea cakes..."

"Good heavens, that *is* boring," she replied with mock horror. "How does anyone find a match with conversations as dull as those? I should think marriage requires an understanding built upon something more substantial than weather and tea cakes."

He frowned. "I thought you weren't looking for marriage."

She lifted her chin. "We established *you* were not."

His fingers tightened possessively. He tried to relax them. She was free to do as she pleased. "So you are on the hunt?"

"It's complicated," she admitted. "And, as you may have noticed, not going very well."

He lowered his voice conspiratorially. "I think everyone has noticed."

He smiled at the eye roll she did not quite manage to hide. He did not smile at the twist to his stomach upon the news she was on the hunt for a husband.

Not that he was available, he reminded himself. Good lord. What should have been an unremarkable waltz was becoming much more dangerous than he could have dreamed.

He put a bit more distance between them. Tried to, anyway. "Do you dance often in America?"

"Never."

"Then how did you learn to waltz?"

"My grandparents hired a tutor when I arrived in London."

Grandparents! His lungs expanded with pleasure. He should not feel so victorious at having teased another personal detail from that rosy mouth but, well, there it was. Although, come to think of it, he hadn't learned much. If there was no dancing in America, why would her grandparents have hired an instructor? And if her grandparents were British, what had she been doing in America? "Where do—"

"York!" came a familiar voice at Oliver's back as the last strains of the waltz faded away. "Introduce me to your friend."

The owner of the deep voice had to know that Miss Halton had not yet made any friends. Oliver turned to flash a cold smile at the Duke of Ravenwood. He was not a friend either. Not anymore. The war had changed them both for different reasons, and neither of them much liked who the other had become.

"It's Carlisle now," Oliver corrected, his voice low and dangerous.

Ravenwood flinched, as if the slight had been accidental rather than premeditated. "That's right. I was very sorry to hear the news. The two of you weren't close, but... A father is a father."

Oliver glared at him in silence. Anything said now would be disastrous to them both.

Ravenwood turned his gaze toward the siren Oliver still hadn't relinquished. "Does this delightful young lady have a name?"

Oliver released Miss Halton's hand. Their moment was clearly over. "Miss Halton, this is His Grace, the Duke of Ravenwood. Ravenwood, this is Miss Halton, of America."

Ravenwood lifted Miss Halton's gloved hand to his parted lips. "The honor—and utter delight—are most assuredly mine, my dear lady. May I have the pleasure of your company during the next set?"

Oliver kept his fists at his sides. The giant stick up Ravenwood's arse would keep him from putting Miss Halton's honor in any danger. And it was time to slip back into the library and check on Xavier. Perhaps he would finally come around.

Miss Halton, for her part, was gazing at Ravenwood, her eyes filled with suspicion, not seduction. Very wise. She'd gone from no dances at all, to being on the arm of both an earl and a duke in quick succession.

The gaggle of nervous young bucks lining up behind them for a chance to add their names to her dance card? Also Oliver's fault. When he'd sought to save Miss Halton's precarious reputation from the evil of wagging tongues, he'd acted as Oliver York, rescuer of people who wished he'd leave them alone. In the heat of the moment, he'd forgotten that he was now the Earl of Carlisle, as well as a decorated war hero whom these dandified imeciles had been emulating from the moment Oliver strode back ashore.

Having won both Ravenwood's and Oliver's attentions, Miss Halton would no longer be in want of dance partners.

Ravenwood passed Miss Halton's dance card to the next addlepate in line, but was not so quick to release her hand. "However did you meet an old caterpillar like Carlisle?"

Oliver's smile froze as he flashed Miss Halton a warning look. He knew they should've gotten their stories straight when they'd had the chance.

She blinked up at Ravenwood innocently. "Didn't he tell you? We've known each other a shocking length of time. If you can credit it, Lord Carlisle is even the first man I ever danced with."

Ravenwood shot a surprised glance at Oliver, who was struggling not to smile at Miss Halton's clever response. Every word was true, yet gave the impression they'd known each other for ages. Which, given that he and Ravenwood had known each other all their lives, would mean Oliver had been keeping her a secret for decades. Splendid idea, that. He wished she *were* his secret. He found himself quite disinclined to share.

He grinned at Miss Halton until the butterflies in his stomach churned into nausea. He was sinking fast. With a gallant bow, he broke free of her web and forced himself to walk away from those enchanting green eyes. Far, far away.

He could not dare risk his heart.

Chapter Four

The next morning, after giving up on deciphering the incoherent handwriting in his father's innumerable estate journals, Oliver tied his horses on Threadneedle Street for a meeting with his father's banker. He had returned home in mid-December but hadn't been able to secure an appointment until after Christmastide. It was just as well, he supposed. He'd needed those few weeks to adjust to the loss of his father and the disorientation of being back in England after three long years at war.

He'd missed the probate proceedings altogether, and his father's solicitors—whomever they might be—had disappeared before Oliver returned home. He was wholly alone.

When he'd been cleaning weapons or charging across battlefields, he'd dreamed of the idle carelessness of his old life. Boxing matches at Gentleman Jackson's. Quick afternoon visits to Tattersall's to bid on the latest horseflesh. Lazy evenings at the pleasure gardens or in bed with his mistress.

But he hadn't come home to any of those things. Hadn't even thought about them since the moment he held his father's coronet in his knife-scarred hands. Leading troops was so much simpler than managing an

earldom. Soldiers were trained. Heirs were...
accidental.

He had come to London determined to make the
best of it. Being back in the city meant Oliver finally
had a chance to find someone capable of explaining the
earldom to him in the King's English. Or at the very
least, make sense of the charts of accounts. He strode
into the Bank of England with his shoulders back and
his head held high.

Unfortunately, the portly Mr. Brown couldn't seem
to make sense of Oliver's presence in his office.

"Young... Master... York?" he gasped, sounding as
if he'd perhaps swallowed a pheasant.

"It's Carlisle now," Oliver found himself explaining
for the second time in as many days. "I'm sure the bank
received notice of my father's unfortunate passing?"

"Yes... Yes... Of course we have done..." Mr.
Brown's feeble reply faded away, but his eyes
remained round as cannonballs.

"Did the accounts not transfer to me, then? Are
there forms I need to sign, evidence to provide?"

"No... Everything is yours, of course. Such that it
is. Of course. I'm just... It's such a surprise that you're
here, that's all. Such a surprise. What with the probate
report, you know."

Oliver shifted in his suddenly uncomfortable chair.
It didn't seem like a good surprise. Nor had he
encountered any reports. His father's financials were a
disaster. "You were not expecting to meet with me?"

"Er, no. Obviously we were not. Meet about what?
In situations like these, that is."

"In situations like what?" Oliver demanded, his
muscles clenched as tight as his jaw. "Situations in
which an heir inherits his father's holdings? My

schedule for the next few weeks is filled with appointments. I'm meeting with everyone in charge of everything. Why wouldn't I meet with the bank?"

"B...because there are no holdings," Mr. Brown stammered. "Your father closed his account with us after he sold the last of the unentailed properties. All that's left is the principle seat. I've no idea how your father was paying his retainers or caring for his tenants these last months." Mr. Brown narrowed his eyes. "Unless there's another account at another bank?"

Another bank? The buzzing in Oliver's ears increased to a roar as his fists tightened painfully. One of the few phrases he'd managed to make out on the first page of each journal was "Bank of England." This could mean only one thing.

"There are no other accounts." The weak voice that scraped from Oliver's hoarse throat didn't sound like his own.

Mr. Brown nodded jerkily, then gave a what-can-you-do lift to his hands. "I'm sorry to hear that, my lord. If that's the case, there's no money. Unless you've funds of your own to invest... ?"

Oliver shook his head. Or tried to. His shoulders were too tight, his neck too corded. He gritted his teeth. Lovely. His father had left the son he'd never wanted alone and penniless. His lips flattened. Checkmate from beyond the grave.

All soldiers left the army with coin in their pockets when they sold their commissions, but Oliver had already spent his on the town house he had rented in Mayfair. There was none left over for salaries or tenants or—good lord, the tailor! The bill he'd accumulated when outfitting Xavier and himself in the first stare of fashion would rival the rents he had paid for his London town house. He gripped the arms of his chair as if he might explode at any moment.

Now what? He couldn't undo all that labor, or make good on any of his debts. The food—where was the food coming from? The tenants, most likely. No wonder his father's liquor supply had dwindled. Oliver had thought the menservants were judging him for going from the battle to the bottle, but there was simply no money left to spend. His breath caught.

The staff! How long would they remain in his employ, once they discovered he could ill afford to keep them? Had they imagined excuses for why their wages were late, expecting the new heir to settle accounts with them at any moment?

His heart raced. He wasn't protecting his tenants, he was stealing from them. And using his servants as free labor until they wised up enough to take themselves to the street. Penniless. Just like him.

He slammed his fist onto the banker's table. Untenable. But what could he do? He didn't have tuppence to wager with at the gaming hells, or much hope of marrying into the kind of fortune he'd need just to break even with debts of this size. An earldom! The Carlisle estate didn't need an heiress, it needed a royal princess. And a magic lantern, just to be safe.

"Why didn't anyone tell me?" No. He tried to rein in his anger. This wasn't Mr. Brown's fault. Blame didn't matter. All of it—every debt, every brick, every tenant—was Oliver's responsibility.

"Your father didn't involve you in his affairs because..." Mr. Brown straightened his documents rather than meet Oliver's eyes. "Frankly, you weren't expected to live."

Oliver leaned forward, startled. "What? When? During the war?"

"When you were born. Your mother died of fever, and you were quite small and sickly."

"Twenty-six years ago! At what point would I be considered healthy enough to be let in on the secret?"

"It's... not secret."

The back of Oliver's neck chilled. "Everybody knew the estate was doomed but me? How is that even possible?"

Mr. Brown shook his head. "The situation didn't become desperate until the final weeks of your father's life. The earldom's lack of funds may not yet be common knowledge, but... Your father couldn't continue to pay his last mistress. Now that he's gone, who knows what pillow talk she'll have with her next protector? If you'll pardon my bluntness."

Shite on a shingle. Mr. Brown's bluntness was the least of Oliver's problems.

His father had died in his final mistress's bed, the infamy of which had vaulted her to the pinnacle of the demimonde. Oliver doubted she'd waited five minutes before sharing every salacious detail with her demimondaine friends, who in turn would do the same with their upper crust clients, and the next thing you knew, all of London will have heard that Oliver's papa didn't just die of prawn salad. He'd died poor. Leaving Oliver the least eligible bachelor in England.

Are your pockets to let? the delectable Miss Halton had asked the night before. Was that an innocent question, or was the truth becoming known?

No, he reminded himself. He hadn't introduced himself yet, so there was no way Miss Halton had matched his face to any rumors.

He hoped.

Oliver pushed himself up on stiff legs and blindly made his way out of the bank and onto the street. He had wasted enough of Mr. Brown's time. And his own.

The past few months had been one nightmare after another. He'd lost his father, his best friends. So much death in so little time.

At least he had no dependents to care for. The four soldiers had marched off as free men and returned home avowed to stay that way. Except for Edmund, who hadn't returned at all. Thank God the man hadn't married his childhood sweetheart before heading into battle. Sarah Fairfax was far too young to be a widow. Not that anything lessened the pain.

Come to think of it, Oliver hadn't seen Miss Fairfax even once since he'd returned to Town. His heart twisted. Although a fiancée wasn't expected to don widow's weeds for a full year like a wife would, he wouldn't be surprised to learn Sarah Fairfax had done. Oliver himself would probably never remove his black armband.

They'd all lost too much.

He crossed his arms and shivered against the January cold. He could pay her a call, check in. A friendly face would be welcome right about now, and they could both use a break from their misery. He couldn't recover an earldom in one day. Spending the afternoon with someone who didn't expect him to be anyone but himself sounded divine.

As he swung up into his carriage, he decided his second errand after Miss Fairfax's town house ought to be finding a stable to take his barouche and his prized pair of grays off his hands. Were there any other horses or carriages to sell, or had his father already rid himself of the lot? His arms broke out in gooseflesh. Perhaps even the greys would not bring in enough blunt to staunch the flow.

How many servants could Oliver let go without the house falling down about his ears? His cheeks burned at what they must think. Some of the staff had been with his family for generations. Their great-grandparents had shined boots and curled hair for Oliver's great-grandparents. He would write glorious letters of recommendation for all of them, but how could he ever repay them for staying as long as they had with no pay? By tossing them to the gutters with nothing more than a spare pair of clothes and a note of commendation in their pockets?

Chapter Five

Berkeley Square, at last! Oliver leapt from his carriage. He had never been so happy to see Sarah Fairfax's gated garden in his life. He needed something, anything, to take his mind off of his impossible situation, even for a few hours.

He made good use of the brass knocker. Within seconds the door cracked open, revealing an inch and a half of the Fairfax butler's familiar face. He did not miss the flash of pain in the butler's eyes.

Oliver frowned. Primble had never hesitated to throw the door wide for any of the five friends. Yet he continued to block the way. Oliver rubbed the base of his neck as he waited for an invitation that was obviously not forthcoming.

"What is it? Is Miss Fairfax unwell?" His throat went dry. He pushed past the butler, despite any risk of contagion to himself. A humorless smile curled his lips. What risk? He'd already planned not to continue the family line. A timely demise was probably the best he could do for the Carlisle estate. "Sarah? Are you ill? It's Oliver. Where are you?"

Hesitant shuffles sounded from behind a tri-paneled embroidered screen. After a fraught moment of silence, she threw herself, sobbing, into Oliver's arms.

Er, sort of. They were separated by an extra
fourteen inches of… belly.

He stared at the top of her head in dawning horror.
Pregnant. No wonder he hadn't seen her about Town.
She couldn't leave her home. This was a hundred times
worse than simple mourning. This was—

"Edmund's baby," she choked out brokenly,
looking up at him with huge bloodshot eyes above
puffy black circles. She probably hadn't slept since she
got the news. Either piece of news.

Bloody hell.

"How—? When—?"

"Bruges," she supplied, smiling through her tears.
"He had one day of leave shortly before you were all
sent to Waterloo, so I met him in Bruges. It's supposed
to be the Venice of Belgium, and it's ever so lovely.
Edmund and I… Edmund and I… We were to be
married!" She wrenched herself from Oliver's arms and
thumped down onto the closest chair, her sobs in her
throat and her face in her hands. "I was meant to have
him forever, and now all that I'll ever have is his
bastard baby!"

"Don't—" *talk like that*, he had been about to say.
But she was right. Damn. He thought back. They'd
gone to Waterloo in early June, and it was now early
January. Seven months. Sarah Fairfax was unwed and
pregnant by a dead man. At two-and-twenty, her life
was over. Oliver sank into the chair opposite her and
reached for her hands. "Who knows?"

"The servants, of course. My parents. And now
you." She glanced up at him with a wry smile. "Why?
Are you going to offer for me? Another couple months
and I'll have one pip of a dowry."

Oliver groaned. The only thing keeping him from doing exactly that—rescuing his best friend's pregnant bride by whisking her to the closest altar—was that he couldn't be assured of a roof over his own head in two months' time, much less be able to provide for a grieving widow and a newborn child. He released Miss Fairfax's hands.

He wasn't like Ravenwood, who believed marriage was only for couples in love. Balderdash. Oliver had never experienced love of any sort. He well understood that life demanded one be more pragmatic than idealistic. So did Miss Fairfax, or she wouldn't have made her jest-that-wasn't-wholly-a-jest. She'd known Oliver her whole life. Rushing in to save her was exactly the sort of thing he was prone to do. This time, however, his hands were tied.

Wait a minute. His foot began to bounce in excitement. Ravenwood was the answer!

That stick-in-the-mud was flush with blunt. He probably stuffed his mattresses with pound notes. Ravenwood might not give Oliver the time of day, but he could be trusted to keep a secret. With a small loan, Miss Fairfax could take an unplanned holiday in the countryside. Sarah was too proud to accept charity but once Ravenwood agreed to help, Oliver would do his damnedest to convince her. If she gave the baby away somewhere far in the north, London would never be the wiser.

His blood rang with excitement. Perfect! If he could convince her to take the money—and Ravenwood to offer it—Sarah could have her old life back by this time next year. Oliver tilted his head toward her, but something stilled his tongue.

She had stopped crying. Her eyes and cheeks were still red and every part of her body swollen, but her breaths quieted as her fingers curved over her round stomach.

It... twitched?

She glanced up at him with a little disbelieving laugh. "Hiccoughs, Oliver! The little scamp is bouncing about my belly with *hiccoughs*."

Oliver's answering smile was more automatic than genuine. Once again, he was too late to save her. Miss Fairfax would never give away Edmund's baby. She would never have her old life back.

None of them would.

Chapter Six

The morning after Grace had danced with the Duke of Ravenwood and the Earl of Carlisle—whose offhand confession that he'd preferred being plain Mr. Oliver York had sounded surprisingly sincere—flowers began to fill the parlor. But the only bouquet she'd clutched to her thumping heart was also the simplest, and the only blooms to arrive without an accompanying note. She didn't need a signature to know whom they were from.

Jasmine. Same as her bath soap. She buried her face in the blossoms and smiled.

Lord Carlisle was off her list of potential husbands, of course. Wrong for her at every turn. Titled. Ex-soldier. She wouldn't be able to trick him into letting her go, nor manipulate him into thinking it was a good idea. He was too smart for that. Too strong. Too sure of himself. She smiled despite herself. He had every reason to be arrogant. He was handsome. Clever. King Triton, surrounded by a sea of guppies.

Worse, she *liked* him. He looked into her eyes and saw more than she wanted him to see. She might not want to let a man like that go, and she definitely wouldn't wish to hurt him.

No, her plans had not changed. If anything, her resolve had doubled. She needed a malleable, forgettable, not-too-bright suitor, who wouldn't mind waking up without his bride. From the dozens of vases peppering the parlor, she'd even managed to pluck a number of possibilities.

The next step was seeing how quickly she could bring one of her maybes up to scratch. One week? Two?

She hated being this desperate. If her grandparents had half a heart, they would send for their sick daughter themselves, rather than waste precious time forcing Grace to dangle from their strings. All they ever said was, *if your mother wants our forgiveness, she can come beg for it herself.* How? Mama was so sick she couldn't make a pot of coffee, much less sail across the ocean! But Grace's pleas fell on deaf ears.

Not for the first time, she fervently wished her father were still alive. For her mother's sake, and for her own. Grace had just started to toddle when he'd been violently stolen from them. She'd been so young that she couldn't recall his face, his smell, his laugh. It wasn't fair. Nothing in life was fair. All she could do was get married, get the money, and take the first boat home. Back to a place where nobody laughed at her manners or her accent. Back to her friends, her life, and her mother.

At the next soirée, Grace spent the first half hour conspicuously sipping a glass of punch in strategic locations throughout the gathering, giving her targets plenty of opportunity to solicit a spot on her dance card. Not that she planned to do much dancing. She didn't have time to fritter away on actual fun.

There was no way to know which suitor was the most viable without conversing with each of them. She intended to spend each set taking turns about the frigid garden until she froze solid.

Taking strolls about the ballroom would be warmer, but much less private. Chaperonage was fine—welcome, actually—but she didn't need the gossips overhearing her nosy questions about the state of each gentleman's pocketbook, or how quickly they could envision themselves at the altar, or if the wife could be presumed to give him the freedom of his own pursuits thereafter.

After an hour and a half of wracking shivers and chattering teeth, Grace could no longer feel her toes. Or her fingers. Or her nose. She was forced to spend the fourth set indoors. It was a country-dance, which would waste an interview opportunity but at least let her stamp a bit of sensation back into her frozen feet. She rubbed her arms and took her place next to Mr. Isaac Downing, who she hoped might become a suitor.

Another wallflower, a bluestocking named Jane Downing, had invited Grace to tea the day before. Upon hearing they would both be attending the same soirée, Miss Downing's elder brother had politely asked if she might save him a dance. This was Grace's chance to see if his interest was more than merely polite, without probing so hard that she alienated her sole potential friend in the entire country.

Due to the interchanging nature of the swirling pairs upon the dance floor, she would only be able to speak to him in hasty snatches before the steps required him to briefly partner the female of the pair opposite them.

Which was distracting enough without the corresponding male being the Earl of Carlisle.

He forbore the pleasantries. "Dance card full, I see."

"So it is." She kept her practiced smile in place despite the thumping of her heart. If he smelled the scent of her jasmine soap upon her skin, would he know she had thought of nothing but him during her bath?

His eyes darkened as he scowled at the list of signatures dangling from her wrist. "My name isn't on your card."

"Very astute." Her breath quickened as his hand tightened around her waist. He couldn't possibly be jealous. If he had any idea how much she wished his name were the *only* one on her dance card...

"Tell me, Miss Halton. Have you seen Ravenwood?"

"What?" Grace's feet stumbled in her confusion. She'd thought Lord Carlisle consumed with envy, when who he'd truly wished to see was the Duke of Ravenwood?

Lord Carlisle lifted her wrist for a better view of her dance card. "Is the rotter on your list or not?"

"No, I..." She meant to pull her wrist away, truly she did. But the heat in Lord Carlisle's eyes when he learned she would not be in Lord Ravenwood's arms held her captive. "I haven't seen him."

"If he crosses your path, tell him I'm looking for him."

"Why do—"

But the pairs were already switching in time with the music, and now she was back to her original partner. Mr. Downing had seemed handsome enough when they'd first crossed paths, but dancing with him after having been in Lord Carlisle's arms was like comparing a vivid oil painting to an insipid watercolor.

Not that it mattered. Grace was hunting marriage, not passion. And so far, this was her best lead.

Mr. Downing's gaze met hers only briefly. "Lovely weather, wouldn't you say?"

The unblinking heat in Lord Carlisle's eyes had made Grace forget the rest of the world altogether, but now that she was free of those strong arms, the chill of January once again sank into her bones. "I find it cold, actually. Aren't my fingers icy?"

"Cold, but not drizzly," Mr. Downing continued after a brief pause. His forehead had lined disapprovingly at the mention of her fingers, but quickly smoothed back into proper blandness. "The sun is always a blessing."

"There is no sun," Grace couldn't stop herself from pointing out. "It's after midnight."

"The moon and stars are also blessings, although nighttime can carry a chill." His voice turned contemplative. "I never go anywhere without a thick scarf."

She stared at Mr. Downing in disbelief. Conversations about the weather were as dull as she'd imagined, and Mr. Downing even duller than she'd feared. Well, it didn't signify. All she needed to know was if Mr. Downing might join her at the altar.

"Have you—"

But she was already spinning back to Lord Carlisle.

"Your fingers are still cold," he said without preamble. "I don't like it."

Her throat made a sound somewhere between a laugh and a cry. "I suppose you would know how to warm them?"

His smile was slow and sinful, and his gaze never left hers. "I am a man of many talents."

The wicked promise in his eyes sent a flutter of heat straight to her belly. She should not encourage him. A flirtation could lead nowhere. Worse, any hint of scandal could ruin any hope of finding a malleable husband. "The weather—"

"—is boring. Did you like my flowers?"

"No."

He shrugged. "To be expected."

She dipped her head, then forced herself to look up at him. "I loved them."

This time she had the pleasure of leaving him the one without a reply as the country-dance spun her back to Mr. Downing. It took her a moment to recall her list of questions to mind. She reaffixed her placid smile.

"Do you come from a large family, Mr. Downing?"

"No. It's just Jane and me."

Excellent. A dearth of relatives would help to keep his expenses low, and a sister meant he did not lack for companionship. "You both enjoy the Season?"

"Jane and I are not enthusiasts of drink or dance, but we try to leave our libraries now and again."

Not being one for drink put Mr. Downing head and shoulders above the others. Grace had hated alcohol ever since her father's death, but the *ton*'s blood seemed to run on port and brandy. Had she any plans to stay beyond the wedding, not dancing with her husband would've been a disappointment. As it stood, Mr. Downing was a wonderful candidate.

But the music returned her to Lord Carlisle. He pinned her with his gaze.

"Your smiles don't reach your eyes tonight. Is something amiss?" The corner of his mouth lifted. "Besides my lack of social graces?"

She frowned up at him. He should not be able to read her this well. She could scarcely admit her intention to marry and flee home, so gave him part of the truth. "I'll be going back to America before too long. I was just thinking about the voyage home. Three weeks in a tiny shared cabin on a passenger ship."

He pulled a face. "I don't mind cramped spaces, but sailing to and from the Continent very nearly killed me. I'll never again cross so much as a river in anything less than a sturdy carriage on a nice solid bridge."

"Seasickness?" she asked with sympathy.

His shudder did not appear feigned. "There's seasickness, and there's *seasickness*. If I were Catholic, they would have administered the last rites. I was less afraid of enemy fire than of undertaking the return trip to England." His eyes were warm but serious. He gave her hand a quick squeeze. "You made it here. You can make it home."

Grace thought back to those long weeks at sea. Her shoulders relaxed. He was right. She had been ill, but not deathly so. Once she had her dowry money in hand, she would have no problem getting back to her mother. Things were going to work out.

"Thank you." She smiled up at him. "Talking to you has made me feel much better."

He affected a haughty accent. "A gentleman cannot accept thanks for simply being a gentleman."

"You?" she teased. "A gentleman?"

He wiggled his eyebrows. "I certainly do not have to be. If the lady prefers, I will happily accept gratitude in the form of kissing me senseless."

She would've *kicked* him senseless if they weren't in the middle of the dance floor. Or perhaps kissed him. If he kept inciting her to violent passions, she could not be held accountable for her reactions. Especially when he always seemed to know just what to say. Her eyes focused on his mouth. He *was* a gentleman. If their situations had been different, she would have liked very much to have those sensual lips press against hers...

Then Mr. Downing reached for her and Lord Carlisle was gone.

Mr. Downing's eyes gazed somewhere over her shoulder. "The cucumber cakes were lovely tonight, wouldn't you agree?"

She shuddered. *Cucumber* and *cake* didn't belong in the same sentence. "I'm afraid I didn't have opportunity to try them."

"The ham was quite gorgeous, as well. Very thinly sliced. Almost transparent."

"Positively ghostly," she murmured.

"The punch was a bit warm for my taste, however." His lips pursed. "Though I suppose it always is."

Fascinating as this line of talk was, Grace needed to steer them back to the primary interview. At this point, she'd take the first viable suitor she could get. She leaned closer to Mr. Downing. "Do you think your life would be greatly changed if you were to marry?"

He looked surprised. "Change how? I wouldn't marry a woman who sought to disrupt my solitude or my schedule."

Grace nodded once, more because she found his answer satisfactory than because she agreed with him. But before she could ask another probing question, he twirled her back into Lord Carlisle's arms.

"I'm not supposed to be in your *arms*," she hissed up at him. "This is a country-dance, not a waltz."

He drew her closer. "And yet I notice you do not pull away."

"Humph." He had her there. "Why are you looking for Ravenwood?"

"Why have you spent the evening in the company of so many imbeciles? Every time I turn around, it's a prance in the garden here, a country-dance there."

"I'm trying to determine if they *are* imbeciles." She raised her chin. Yet something made her want to confide in him. "If you must know, I'm screening potential suitors."

"Oh? You didn't invite me to the garden. Or give me a chance to ask you to dance." The ferocity of his scowl melted her knees.

"You've made it clear you're not looking to wed." She arched her brows. "Besides, I already know we won't suit. Do you disagree?"

He held her gaze.

She held her breath.

And then Mr. Downing swung her back to his side.

"It certainly feels like January," he said, his voice as placid as his expression. "Are you looking forward to the Season?"

It was the first personal question he'd asked her. Perhaps that was why she answered so honestly. "No."

He tilted his head. "I never do, either. I promise, I have tried."

She bit her lower lip. Might he also be sizing her up as a potential wife? "What other hobbies do you enjoy?"

"Reading, mostly. I don't garden because plants make me sneeze." He frowned. "Are you a lover of flowers, Miss Halton?"

He *was* sizing her up as a future Mrs. Downing!

"No," she lied quickly. "Books are far more favorable. They don't… wilt."

Mr. Downing beamed at her happily. "What authors are you currently reading?"

Her eyes widened, but the music saved her from having to invent names. In the space of a heartbeat, her hand was back in Lord Carlisle's.

"Yes," he said abruptly.

She stared at him. "Yes, what?"

"Yes, I disagree with your assessment." By the set of his jaw, he was displeased he'd even mentioned it. But now that he had, he wouldn't back down. "We would obviously suit."

Her breath caught in her throat. Yes! *No*. That is—

"But I can't marry you." He glanced away, and put a more respectable distance between them. "I'm sorry."

"I can't marry you either," she said much too loudly. Informing herself as much as him. His rejection stung. Who cared what his reasons were? She had reasons of her own. There was nothing to feel disappointed about. No reason at all for the empty feeling in her stomach or the urge to burrow back into his arms.

His next words were so soft she almost missed them.

"But I would've enjoyed it."

He flung her back to Mr. Downing before she could do something foolish like shred her entire dance card in order to spend the rest of the evening with Lord Carlisle. January or not, she had no doubt he would ensure every part of her body stayed warm as they strolled the garden. More importantly, he seemed to connect with her on a level far deeper than the physical. He *cared*.

The country set ended without giving her another opportunity to return to Lord Carlisle's arms. She might have rushed to his side, had Mr. Downing not saved her from herself. Ever proper, he did not abandon her until

Mr. Leviston, the next suitor on her card, came to take her arm.

As they headed out to the garden, Grace meant to run through every question on her potential suitor list— truly, she did—but found herself asking about the Earl of Carlisle instead.

Mr. Leviston's brow creased. "Carlisle? Stay away from that one. He needs more blunt than an empire of textile factories could provide. Hear he's on the lookout for an heiress."

Lord Carlisle had lied to her? She hugged herself. "How do you know?"

"Poor mug just found out his father spent the family fortune on whor—on evening entertainment. He's near to blown up at Point Nonplus, as they say. Just yesterday, Carlisle sold all but the scrawniest of his horses and most of his carriages. Wanted to get my hands on his matched grays, but some blackguard beat me to it."

Grace couldn't hide her shock. Her relief at not having been lied to paled next to the horror of Lord Carlisle finding himself penniless because his father had wasted his future on whores. And yet Lord Carlisle made no complaint. Instead, he'd noted *her* unhappiness, regardless of her being too wrapped up in herself to note his own.

Despite being desperate enough to unload his remaining possessions on acquaintances that would obviously gossip, he still put her peace of mind before his own worries.

She swallowed hard. She wished she *could* marry him. But if he was reduced to selling off horses, he needed far more than her dowry could provide. Even if she were in the position to let him have it all, one thousand pounds was nowhere near enough to save a destitute earldom.

"What's he going to do?"

"Got bets on that at White's. Most obvious thing would be to get rid of the Black Prince, but someone would have to pry that portrait out of Carlisle's cold dead hands."

"Black... Prince?"

"Oh, right. You're American." Mr. Leviston tapped his chin as he considered his explanation. "The Black Prince is more rightfully known as Edward of Woodstock, Prince of Wales, Duke of Cornwall, and Prince of Aquitaine. King Edward III made him the first duke in England, almost five hundred years ago."

"Why would Lord Carlisle care about that?"

"They're cousins. Or so the story goes. His father— old Carlisle—used to drag every person who crossed his threshold into the family Hall of Portraits. Had the Black Prince hanging right there where his son's face ought to be. Only painting in the entire gallery framed in gold, although it wouldn't really matter. Canvas like that would be valuable no matter what."

She recoiled at the injustice. "Why on earth wasn't it the first thing Lord Carlisle got rid of? It sounds horrid. I can't imagine hanging onto something like that."

"Then you're not as sentimental as Carlisle. His land is entailed, and that painting might as well be." At her blank expression, Mr. Leviston shook his head. "American, right. Entailed means he legally can't get rid of his land, because it belongs to the title, not to the person. Carlisle would never sell that portrait. It's hung in the family gallery ever since the paint first dried. Trust me, I heard the story from Carlisle's father a thousand times. Can't blame the Black Prince. Not his fault old Carlisle was a terrible father."

"I'm glad he's dead," she blurted. "Let him go be with his Black Prince if he loved him so much."

"Family," Mr. Leviston said with a shrug. "Can't pick 'em."

How true. Grace's shoulders caved inward. She couldn't even pick the husband she wanted.

Chapter Seven

"Higher, if you please, *mademoiselle*."

Grace lifted her arms into the air. She forced herself to smile at her grandmother over the top of the latest modiste's head. It was not their fault that Grace wasn't enjoying being pinned and measured and fitted. She didn't feel like a story princess at all. In the beginning, she couldn't help but be dazzled by the sweeping gowns and candlelit ballrooms, but she would trade it in a heartbeat for the money to go rescue her mother.

Trade it all. Her mouth twisted. If only she could. But everything within sight belonged to her grandparents. Even if they gifted her this trousseau, it wouldn't help. There were exclusive venues throughout London dedicated to the sale and resale of diamonds or racing horses, but not for gowns. They might be expensive to design and custom fit, but were hardly a premium commodity. Who would Grace sell her used clothes to, even if she could? Her lady's maid?

Grandmother Mayer nodded at the modiste approvingly. "She's going to look splendid. Just as beautiful as her mother did during her come-out. She cannot fail to make a fine match."

Somehow, Grace kept a determined smile fixed on her face. She didn't want to look splendid. She wanted to be halfway back to America. But since she had to marry in order to achieve that goal, she was determined not to ruin her grandmother's excitement any more than she had to. The woman was under no legal obligation to clothe and feed her, much less provide a dowry. Grace was quite conscious of her tenuous fortune.

Although they had been complete strangers when she appeared on the Mayers' doorstep a little over a week ago, her grandparents had welcomed her into their homes... and had been furious that her mother had stayed behind. No matter how many times Grace explained that her mother was back in Pennsylvania because she was literally too ill to even rise from bed, her grandparents wouldn't believe a word of it. They were convinced that Grace's presence was nothing more than a scheme to run back to America with a portion of the Mayers' money.

Because her grandparents refused to be taken advantage of in such a nefarious manner, they gave her no pin money of her own and never left her alone with so much as a piece of cutlery.

Grace didn't even have the right to be offended. She *was* here because she wanted money, and she absolutely intended to abscond with it at the first opportunity. Her grandparents were wrong about Grace's reasons, but right to be suspicious. She hadn't diminished their misgivings by reminding them that she only intended to take advantage of her future husband.

That was another score on which they failed to see eye-to-eye.

Grace needed to marry someone who didn't need her. Someone with enough money and mistresses that they wouldn't miss her or the dowry once she was gone. She intended to return, of course. She would dishonor neither holy matrimony nor her husband by disappearing for good. Her stomach twisted at the thought of abandoning a husband so soon after the wedding.

But that was why she needed to marry someone who wouldn't trouble himself over a brief separation. Her mother needed her, and Mama came first.

Grandmother Mayer, on the other hand, wanted Grace to become the toast of the *ton*. She said Grace's striking looks and unconventional background would make her an Original, and put her on the path to becoming a duchess, or perhaps even catching the eye of some foreign prince.

The flowers accumulating in the front parlor only exacerbated her grandmother's mania. She was determined Grace would marry well. Not just because of Grandmother Mayer's blatant frustration that her own upward mobility had peaked, no matter how much money she and her husband amassed. Not even because she saw in Grace the opportunity to make the sort of match she'd always dreamed of for her own child.

Worse. Grandmother Mayer truly believed that Grace and a besotted suitor joining hands at the altar would be the only enticement capable of inducing her coldhearted, money-hungry, not-remotely-sick mother into hopping onto a boat and crossing the Atlantic Ocean.

Upon which, what precisely was supposed to happen? Mama and Grandmother Mayer would fall tearfully into each other's arms? Duel at dawn? Attack each other with parasols? Grace had no idea, and she doubted her grandmother did, either. She spoke of her daughter with disdain and contempt and bitterness, and yet wished more than anything for her return.

But all she got was Grace.

Grandmother Mayer didn't love her unexpected granddaughter, or even particularly like her. She didn't even bother to try to get to know her. Grace wasn't family, but rather a means to an end. She certainly wasn't interested in Grace's impassioned pleas of sickness and urgency. She was too busy scheming about how she might get Grace into Almack's.

"When we're done with the fitting, may I go to Hyde Park with Miss Downing?" she asked quietly.

Grandmother Mayer's sharp gray eyes snapped toward Grace. "Why?"

Grace bit back a sigh. Since arriving, she hadn't been allowed to leave the Mayers' residence unless she was en route to a location her grandmother chose, dressed as her grandmother wished, seen by those her grandmother sought to impress. Every other moment was spent with dance instructors, etiquette tutors, fashion plates... anything that might help a gauche American become more attractive to those who mattered. Perhaps the Duke of Ravenwood or the Duke of Lambley, her grandmother suggested often. Sometimes the pressure was more than Grace could stand.

For the moment, all she wanted was a friendly face. Somewhere far from her grandmother's watchful eye. Somewhere she wouldn't be expected to flirt or simper.

Of course, saying something like that aloud was the quickest way to get stuffed back into her room until Candlemas. She had to try a different tack.

"The ladies promenade there every afternoon, and the gentleman ride by on their curricles. Miss Downing says it's the best place to see and be seen."

Her grandmother frowned. So far, Grace had only been permitted to attend balls and soirees. Locations where music and dancing might help ensnare the heart of a Corinthian. Her grandmother's skeptical look indicated this pattern was unlikely to change.

"Both Carlisle and Ravenwood will be there," Grace rushed to add. "And many other dukes and earls." She had no idea if this was true, but if they did *not* show, Grandmother Mayer could hardly blame their absence on Grace. "Perhaps one of the *haut ton* will become hopelessly enamored."

This, at last, proved too much temptation. "Very well. Take your maid. I won't have you damaging your reputation. I've worked hard to bring respectability back to the Mayer name." Grandmother frowned. "I do want you to succeed, Grace. Your triumph is my triumph. Seeing you well-matched may not undo the mistakes of the past, but it will improve our futures. I cannot manipulate the *ton* for you. To do that, you must take care to stay on your very best behavior."

Grace nodded. To most of society, one's reputation was even more important than one's dowry. The last thing she needed was to make it harder to snare a husband. She already had her dowry spent.

The smallest piece of the pie was the return ticket home. Two more tickets would be required to return with Mama, but first was whatever doctors and medicines she needed to get well. If it looked like it might take months for her mother to return to full health, she would have to fortify their home. There were a hundred repairs to be made to the little shack, not to mention clothes to darn, food to eat... A thousand-pound dowry seemed a princely sum when she had first learned of it, but she now worried it would barely get her mother back on her feet.

"*C'est tout*," announced the modiste, plucking a pin from Grace's hem. "You are finished, *mademoiselle*."

Grace lowered her aching arms with a grateful smile. "Thank you."

Grandmother Mayer's gave a brisk nod. "You may send your bill to Mr. Mayer once you've completed all the new gowns. We'll need the first within a week."

The modiste nodded quickly. "As you please. I thank you for—"

Before the modiste could finish speaking, Grandmother Mayer was out of Grace's dressing room and gone.

The modiste dipped an awkward curtsey in Grace's direction and hurried out into the hall after her patroness.

Grace turned to her lady's maid, who was picking stray pins from the floor. "Will you accompany me to Hyde Park, Peggy?"

The girl glanced up from her task only long enough to cut a flat-eyed stare in Grace's direction before returning her gaze to the carpet. "If you wish."

Grace sighed. Normally, the upper class would inform, rather than invite, their servants. But Grace had been part of that world for less than two weeks, and she still wasn't used to other people doing things for her. Her hesitancy showed.

Peggy, for her part, only did the bare minimum required. She ensured Grace was dressed and untangled the occasional knot from her hair, but they certainly weren't forming any sort of bond. Perhaps it was Grandmother Mayer's tendency to speak of Grace like an object—or not at all. Or perhaps it was simply the ignominy of being forced to wait upon someone with absolutely no claim to aristocracy. Or even money.

Unlike Grace, Peggy was *used* to living in a grand house and wearing pretty dresses and eating delicious meals. It wasn't that the maid thought herself above her station. It was that she didn't believe Grace to deserve *hers*.

Problem was, Peggy was right. Grace didn't belong in high society. Or in England. She missed the simplicity of her life back in Pennsylvania, and she deeply missed her mother. But the only way to get her mother back was to continue with this charade and shackle herself to the first suitor with enough coin that he wouldn't miss Grace's modest dowry.

She pulled a spencer from her wardrobe and shoved her arms into the sleeves. Someone *might* give her a second glance. Perhaps today would be the day she managed to turn an admirer into a suitor.

Peggy followed at a respectable, if lackluster distance as Grace hurried downstairs to have one of her grandparents summon a carriage. She found them in a sitting room, enjoying an afternoon tea.

Her grandfather glanced up first, and smiled. "Off to get a beau, are you? Well, you look pretty enough. I shan't be surprised if you summon a passel of proposals by nightfall."

"Better someone else's money than ours," Grandmother Mayer added without looking up from her biscuit. "Your new gowns are costing me twice as much as your dowry. Until you get a suitor, don't ask me for more charity."

Grace's entire body tensed. "For the last time, I am not after your money!"

"I thought you said you wanted a few hundred quid," Grandmother Mayer said around her biscuit. "For your 'sick' mother, of course."

"Yes! Not for personal gain, but for my mother. She *is* sick. Deathly sick. She could use your help."

"Oh, for the love of…" Grandmother Mayer stabbed a fork in Grace's direction. "Your mother isn't sick. She's crafty. Clara sent you so she could get her hands on our money. I know it. You know it. When can we stop playacting?"

Grace's throat clogged with rage. "I am not—"

"I posted a boat ticket the morning you arrived," her grandfather said casually. Both she and her grandmother turned to stare at him.

"You *what*?" Grandmother Mayer demanded, slamming her fork onto the table. "Why bother? Clara swore she'd never step foot back in England."

"Her daughter's here," Grandfather Mayer said simply. "Didn't you say she might return if Grace gets married? She can't swim across the Atlantic. She needs a boat ticket. Just in case she truly is too beggared to buy her own, I went ahead and sent her passage. I got the address from Grace's letter home. I expect to see her before too long."

Grace rubbed her temples. "You didn't send money?"

He shook his head. "No. I sent a ticket. For the best ship I could find."

Grandmother Mayer harrumphed. "More than she deserves. Some of us *work* for our money. She had her chance to make a good match and she squandered it."

"Don't be so hard on the girls," Grandfather Mayer interrupted. "Clara chose love over money because of her youth. Grace isn't silly enough to make *that* mistake. When Clara comes home, I don't want you browbeating her with ancient quarrels. Not when we're so close to being a family again."

Grace's legs trembled. "None of that matters. How is Mama supposed to get to the port and on a boat when she's too sick to get out of bed?"

Grandmother Mayer rolled her eyes skyward. "Stop it. If she were half as sick as you say, you'd never have left her in the first place."

Grace's fingernails bit into her palms. "I had no other choice!"

"Clara is *fine*. She's always fine. This is just another scheme." Grandmother Mayer tossed a pointed look at her husband. "Don't you see? Grace is just as much of a liar as her mother was. I don't feel bad at all about reading those letters."

Grace's blood ran cold. "What letters?"

"The letters your mother wrote you. If I had any doubt about your perfidy, her words proved it."

Grace's mouth fell open. "My mother wrote to me? What did she say? Where are the letters?"

"In the fireplace, along with yours. What does it matter? All she said is that she's fine and hopes you're enjoying England."

"You burned my correspondence?" Grace nearly choked. No wonder her mother had vowed never to return! "You're wrong about Mama. She has to say she's fine. That's what mothers *do*. She'd tell me that with her very last breath."

Grandmother Mayer shrugged and turned back to her tea cakes. "I wouldn't trust either one of you with a sack of beans. Clara ran off the moment our backs were turned, and you've already said that no matter how many gowns and opportunities our money affords you, you fully intend to do the same. Very pretty manners. How do you expect me to react?"

Grace's stomach twisted. "I know it makes me a horrible person for leaving my husband as soon as I have my dowry, but I'll be back as soon as Mama's well enough to come with me and then you'll see—"

Grandmother Mayer gurgled with laughter. "See? That's precisely how I know you're lying. Your mother would never have suggested a plan that foolish. Clara was *born* here. She knows how matrimony works. I can't believe she'd puff you full of empty dreams, just to chase down a penny."

Grace turned her uncomprehending gaze toward her grandfather.

He shook his head. "Your dowry isn't for you, child. It's for your husband. And he's not required to give you a penny of it—now or ever."

Grandmother Mayer lifted her cup of tea in mock salute. "Open your eyes, child. You're never going back to America. I won't buy you a ticket to that godforsaken place and neither will your future husband."

Chapter Eight

By the time Grace alighted in Hyde Park, she was in no mood to engage in mindless flirtations. Unfortunately, her feelings didn't enter into the equation. Even if there had been no reason to rush home to America, she couldn't bear to live under the same roof as her grandparents for even a moment longer.

So she opened her parasol at a jaunty angle, pasted a brittle smile on her face, and stepped in time beside Miss Jane Downing. Hooves clopped merrily by as carriages ambled down Rotten Row. Miss Downing kept up a steady commentary about everyone they passed. The Grenville siblings invited Grace to their next ball. Lady Matilda Kingsley invited her to tea.

Zero gentlemen offered for Grace's hand.

She kept a relentlessly pleasant smile plastered on her face and tried to keep her spirits up. She was going to marry one of these blue bloods if it killed her.

Her mother's life depended on it.

Gravel crunched as a set of carriage wheels slowed to a stop right beside her. She tilted her parasol in order to cast an enquiring glance at the driver. Golden brown eyes twinkled down at her from the narrow, open carriage. Her heart tumbled. *Lord Carlisle*.

He held out his hand. "Take a turn about the park with me?"

She swallowed. Of course she wanted to, despite him being all wrong for her. Earls were disinclined to send their countesses to other continents, never mind that he wouldn't be able to spare a penny. But being seen with him was still advantageous. It made her look desirable to the masses. More importantly, being with him made her *feel* better. He was the only other person she'd come to think of as a friend.

Still, her grandmother's words of warning rang in her ears. There was barely enough space for a second person inside Lord Carlisle's carriage, much less room for Miss Downing and both of their maids. "Thank you for your offer, but I mustn't leave my friend."

"What? *Go.*" Miss Downing made a shooing motion. "The maids and I will still be on the path when you make it back around."

Grace cast her a doubtful look. "But—"

"What have you to fear? It's a *curricle*," Miss Downing pointed out dryly. "Everyone can see both of you, from every angle. Don't be so missish. I should think three hundred chaperones would be plenty."

Well. That was true enough. With a smile, Grace accepted Lord Carlisle's hand and climbed up into the carriage.

After traveling a few yards in silence, he turned to her, his face serious. "Tell me what's troubling you."

She let out a long, shaky breath, no longer surprised at how well he could read her. "My mother. I'm worried about her. She was ill when I left home, and I haven't been in contact with her since."

He frowned. "You phrased that very carefully. By the level of your concern, I assume you have attempted to make contact several times. Are you afraid your mother is too sick to answer?"

He didn't know the half of it. Fury licked through her veins and her fingers shook. "Today I found out that my grandparents have been burning our letters. They disowned my mother years ago when she first left for America. All our correspondence has gone straight into the fire. She must be as sick with worry as I am."

"Use my address," Lord Carlisle ordered without hesitation. "Bring your letters to me. I will frank them. Instruct your mother to direct her replies to my home. Your grandparents cannot touch either of you there."

For a moment, her throat was too prickly to allow proper speech. She nodded, blinking fast, then touched her fingers to his arm. "Thank you."

"Anything you need," he said gruffly.

Her smile turned wistful. She returned her fingers to her lap and interlocked them tight. It would not do to develop an infatuation. And if it were already too late, it definitely would not do to touch his arm and cast sighing gazes at him when they couldn't be less suited for each other.

"What brings you to Hyde Park today?" she asked.

"Scaring up money," he admitted. "I hope to entice some young blade into buying this curricle. It's one of the last of my possessions with any value."

"What about the Black Prince?" she blurted. Her cheeks flushed at the impertinent question. It was one thing to be aware he hadn't a penny to his name. It was another thing altogether to have obviously been listening to gossip. "I'm sorry. I shouldn't have—"

"Someday, I may have to sell him." Lord Carlisle's gaze unfocused toward the horizon. "'Tis the last thing I wish to do. He's been part of my family for generations."

She stared at his shuttered profile. He plainly hated to sell the painting. He'd even referred to the portrait as *he*, rather than *it*. She bit her lip. What a tough situation. If she had the spare coin, she'd buy it herself to make certain he could get it back.

"How about you?" he asked, his eyes sharp. "Just out for a stroll with friends?"

She took a deep breath. If he could be painfully honest, so could she. "Not exactly. I'm trying to tempt a rich bachelor into offering for my hand. Perhaps I can market myself to whoever is interested in your carriage. Buy a coach, get a bride. What do you think?"

"I think you'll get more offers than this curricle will. Any man would be foolish not to want you."

Her heart fluttered. "Well, they'll be foolish if they take me. I'm only getting married because I'm after my own dowry money." She sighed. "Although my grandparents inform me that any future husband is unlikely to hand it over."

Lord Carlisle tilted his head. "I don't know. Technically, the dowry goes to the husband, not the bride. But if you marry someone with deep enough pockets, he wouldn't miss it. Your pin money alone might be more than adequate. What do you need it for?"

"To fetch my mother," she answered immediately. "Well, first to nurse her back to health, and then to bring her to England."

His eyes crinkled sardonically. "To live with the lucky gentleman whom you married for his money?"

Her spine slumped against the carriage. "Despicable plan, isn't it?"

He shrugged. "Seems to be my plan, too. Marrying money, I mean. Not sailing off to America. Even *with* an heiress, I'm unlikely to have so much as a weekend holiday from my estate for many, many years. There's too much work to be done to ensure the solvency and future of the estate. Before it crumbles."

She narrowed her eyes. His words were flippant, but his voice… He hated this, all of it. Of course he did. Inheriting a destitute earldom. Selling the Black Prince. Marrying an unknown heiress.

Her stomach twisted at the image of Lord Carlisle's arms about some horrid princess. Blast. She was beyond infatuated. She *hated* to think of him building a life with someone else. But what was the alternative? Offer to split her small dowry with him if he'd just settle for her instead?

"How much money do you need? For your earldom, I mean." This time, she didn't blush at the impertinent question. She needed to know the answer.

"Ten thousand would be a start," he said wearily. "With that, I could settle debts and ensure all my tenants would survive the winter. Another ten or twenty thousand to make needed repairs and provide for future emergencies. I'd still live on an empty manor with few servants and two ancient horses, but at least I wouldn't feel like I had a noose tightened about my neck."

So much money, just to get started. She swallowed hard. Offering him half of her meager thousand would be ensuring his tenants wouldn't make it through the winter.

Oh, if only she were wealthy! She could save her mother *and* Lord Carlisle. Who cared if they lived on an empty manor with few servants and two ancient horses? She neither wanted nor needed riches. She was *used* to managing a small household with no staff and limited resources. He was possibly the only gentleman of the *ton* for whom she'd actually make a decent bride.

Except for the small matter of her needing to sail to America to save her mother and him needing thirty thousand pounds to rescue his earldom.

She snuck another glance at him from beneath her lashes. He deserved a better life. If that meant that he was destined to marry an heiress, then she should do whatever she could to ensure he met his goal. She might have no connections or sphere of influence, but if she found herself among wealthy young ladies looking to land a title, she could truthfully put him forth as one of the most caring, worthy people of her acquaintance. Perhaps in some small way, she could help him secure a bride.

Even if it ripped her heart in two.

Chapter Nine

Oliver slipped into his father's office. No. *Oliver's* office. Lord knew he worked hard enough for it. More than his father ever did. He let his backside thud into the thick leather chair, then crossed his arms atop the desk and lay down his pounding head for just... one... second.

The last time he'd been this exhausted, he'd spent a week marching on a few hours' sleep per night. Surviving as earl was shaping up to be an even more grueling battle. On even less sleep.

He'd spent the past week in the country with his tenants. Out in their fields. Inside their barns. Up on their roofs. He was lucky that gloves were en vogue, or he'd never be able to hide the scabs and calluses.

And of course he had to hide them. He needed the good regard of the *crème de la crème* of the Upper Ten Thousand. Who else would have both the means and the vicious delight necessary to snap up all of his cherished possessions at ridiculous sums? He'd sold his grays for more than he'd purchased them, just so a loose-tongued dandy could have bragging rights at the next horse race.

Oliver sighed wearily. Most of the rooms in his childhood home were now empty. He'd managed to sell everything of value, except for the daily minimum required for survival... and the family paintings still hanging in the Hall of Portraits. The cursed Black Prince, whom Oliver both loved and hated just as much as he'd loved and hated his father. The Prince was the son his father had wished he'd had, the only face he'd gazed upon.

Fittingly, the Black Prince was still the only thing of value in the entire estate. Oliver had sold everything else.

The servants were scandalized at the stately manor now boasting only a handful of semi-furnished rooms, but they didn't dare voice their concerns. Not when their wages were up-to-scratch for once.

He lifted his head from his crossed arms and tugged an empty journal free from the shelves behind him. Today was the day he began anew. A fresh start.

First thing this morning, he'd ridden all over London, settling past due accounts. He wouldn't have new clothes or fancy cheroots for years—if ever—but at least he'd climbed out of the hole and onto solid ground.

Afterward, he'd skipped lunch to go straight to the bank. Mr. Brown opened a new account in Oliver's name, depositing one third of the small remaining funds therein, and investing the other two thirds in some sort of complicated interest scheme that Oliver wouldn't be able to touch for six months, but was guaranteed not to lose value at least.

Last, he'd stopped by Miss Fairfax's house. He'd waited until the money was out of reach because he didn't want to be tempted into using all of it to save one person, when he still had dozens of servants and a hundred tenants counting on him for their continued well-being.

He didn't mention Ravenwood. Largely because he couldn't find the confounded duke. He hadn't retuned any of Oliver's calls at his estate. And Oliver could hardly add, *"Important—Miss Fairfax is pregnant!"* at the bottom of his calling cards.

Although there was no hope of Sarah giving up the baby, Ravenwood ought to be able to do *something* to ease the way. If Oliver could unearth him. If the duke was never at home, Oliver's only hope was society events. He would attend every last one until the invitations dried up, and if he hadn't found the stodgy bounder by then, he'd pitch a tent on Ravenwood's doorstep and wait him out.

Wouldn't be the first time Oliver slept on the ground. He'd learned all about sleeping in the great out-of-doors while serving in the army. An achievement unlikely to impress the fops or the ladies, but the five hundred quid in his brand new account wouldn't last forever, and a wise man ought to have a fallback plan in case his house fell down around him.

Not that *My servants and I can always share a lean-to next to the Thames* was much of a fallback plan.

He rubbed his face. No wallowing allowed. There was work to do. He entered the opening details of his new banking account on the first page of the journal, then pushed it to the corner of his desk to dry.

Day One, complete.

Almost.

Fatigued as he was, there was still the Grenville rout yet to attend. All Oliver wished to do was fall into bed for about thirty hours, but too many people were counting on him. Whether they knew it or not. He still had to find Ravenwood and beg him to lend aid to Miss Fairfax. And of course Miss Halton was expecting

Oliver to make good on his promise to frank her letters home to her mother.

Miss Halton. A sudden smile dispelled much of Oliver's exhaustion. Even without a pretext, he'd still be looking forward to seeing her. He loved her quick wit, her fierce loyalty to her mother, the way she made him work for her smiles and laughter.

The thing he'd miss most about society events wouldn't be the extravagant post-theatre meals or the raucous hunting weekends or the sunset promenades on St. James Square. No, what he'd miss most would be those precious stolen moments with Miss Halton.

It wasn't that time stood still when he had her in his arms. It was that nothing else mattered. When her clear green eyes laughed up at him from beneath those arched black brows, the rest of the world simply fell away, and all that he knew was her. The sweet jasmine of her hair. The plumpness of her lower lip. The warm curve of her hip beneath his palm, and the endless desire to pull her closer, to press her to him so that her breasts crushed against his waistcoat as his hungry mouth finally claimed hers. There was nothing he wanted more than to taste her, to make her his own...

Madness! He shoved to his feet, furious over his lapse into fancy. She would never be his. He needed an heiress, not Miss Halton. There was no use dreaming about something that could not happen.

Money was running out. A month from now, he'd be lucky to have enough food to keep from starving to death one of these harsh winter nights. Was that the sort of future he wished for Miss Halton? He would rather die himself than cause anyone else to suffer for his father's folly.

The best thing to do, the smart thing to do, was to keep her at arm's length. Frank her letters. Be her friend. Stand aside in the shadows as some other man, some dashing, richer, *better* man swept her off her feet and into a chapel.

His stomach twisted. It took all his will to keep his trembling fists flush at his sides. If he punched a hole in the wall, he could ill afford to repair it. His jaw tightened. Even *that* small avenue of release was now closed to him.

With a sigh, he quit the office and made his way to his bedchamber to ring for a bath. He glared at the bell pull. Soon enough, he'd be hauling buckets of hot water up the stairs himself. Perhaps this very week. Now that he had his head around the Carlisle state of affairs (miserable) there was nothing left but to spend the next several days writing letters of recommendation for his entire staff. They deserved better, and the least he could do was make sure they received it.

In the meantime, however, his aching muscles deeply enjoyed relaxing in hot water he hadn't had to slog up the stairs himself.

He let his valet make as much fuss over the matching of his waistcoat and cravat as the man wished—after all, even if Oliver could somehow afford to keep a valet in his employ, the man's enthusiasm for his task would diminish once he realized his master meant to let his wardrobe fall to rot.

On his way to the front door, Oliver detoured by the office to return the now-dry journal back to its proper place on the shelves. He caught sight of the last two fingers of his father's port in the otherwise empty cupboard where the old earl had once kept the rest of his liquors.

Oliver poured what was left into one of the few remaining wine glasses, and swirled the burgundy liquid beneath his nose. He couldn't afford to buy more, and he wouldn't do so even if he could. This was the last of his father's wine. The last trace of his father anywhere. The spartan office, the empty house, the entire desolate manor estate... it now belonged to Oliver, and Oliver alone.

He could drink to that.

Syrupy and tart, the thick wine danced across his tongue and slid down his throat. He smiled over the rim of the glass. Never had year-old, over-decanted port tasted so sweet. One more swallow and it, too, was nothing more than a memory.

By the time Oliver's aging horse lumbered up to the Grenville estate, the crush was in full swing. The butler called Oliver's name out toward the ballroom, but Oliver doubted anyone registered a word. He could barely hear the butler himself, even from two paces away.

This rout was madness. The Grenvilles must be over the moon.

Oliver checked for Ravenwood in all the usual male haunts, to no avail. Nor was the duke at the buffet, or sipping wine, or twirling a young lady about the dance floor. Oliver pressed his lips together. Whatever that sobersides was up to, it had better be good.

"—just can't understand it," came a familiar voice from somewhere just behind him. "That braying Yankee *accent*!"

God's teeth. Phineas Mapleton. The helpful bigot who'd so fortuitously pointed Oliver toward "Miss Macaroni" a fortnight ago. His veins popped as he clenched and unclenched his fists and tried to slow his racing heart. The best thing to do with a windbag like that was to ignore him, but the blackguard could only be talking about Miss Halton. *Oliver's* Miss Halton. There wasn't a single thing wrong with the lady, and he'd be damned if he'd let Mapleton's spiteful words harm Miss Halton's chances of attracting an eligible suitor. Even if it couldn't be Oliver.

"—I mean, why bother signing her dance card? It's so *public*. And an utter waste of time, since the only thing any of us want to do with the chit is tup her. You can't hear her accent when you've got your Thomas in her mouth. Mine wants to—"

Oliver sailed through the crowd, parting three rows of revelers. His fist crashed directly into Mapleton's teeth.

Music screeched. Dancers stumbled into each other. Impossibly, predictably, the entire pretentious circus came to an utter, gleeful halt.

"Did you *strike* him?" asked one genius.

"Over *Miss Halton*?" exclaimed another.

Mapleton spat blood but smirked up at Oliver. "That light-skirts must have the devil's magic in her cunny for you to—"

A pair of calm but firm hands pulled Oliver away before his fist decided Mapleton ought to lose a few more teeth.

"Stand down, Carlisle," came a low voice at his ear. "What the devil are you about, man? Think of how this looks!"

Ravenwood. The two of them could level Mapleton and all his cronies.

Oliver grabbed the duke's arm. "That rotten knave said the only way to avoid Miss Halton's accent was to—"

"I heard him," Ravenwood continued quietly, "but the orchestra was too loud for his voice to carry."

Oliver broke out into a cold sweat as he realized what the duke was trying to tell him.

Very few people had caught Mapleton's original remarks. Most of the party had seen Oliver attack him from out of nowhere. And in the ensuing silence, every last one of them had heard Mapleton refer to her as a whore, and proclaimed Oliver's carnal relationship with her as the reason behind his outburst. Nausea bubbled in his stomach as his fingers dug into his palms. His spine slumped.

Just once, he'd like one of his bloody rescues to work out right. In attempting to save Miss Halton's reputation... he'd ruined it.

"Lord Carlisle?"

Oliver's fingers went cold. A dangerous tingling sensation prickled across his chest. He turned ever so slowly, forcing his frown to melt away. The sight of Miss Halton's stricken expression slashed into his heart. He'd wished to defend her. Instead, all he'd ensured was that Mapleton's remarks would be repeated over breakfast the next morning, and every day after. Her invitations would soon be to all the wrong sorts of parties. And her suitors... Well. No one respectable would court a woman he believed to be Oliver's seconds.

"Miss Halton." Oliver took a tentative step forward. "I only wanted..." He cleared his throat. "That is, he..." Shite. His stomach sank. "I'm so sorry."

He reached out, but she jerked away from him, her glittering eyes as much hurt as angry. Then she swung her face toward his and sniffed hard.

"Drunk." Her lip curled in disgust.

What on earth? The port. It had only been one glass, but to Miss Halton even a faint scent of wine must be too much, because she was already shaking, already tearing away, already gone.

Oliver didn't pursue her. The scandal would be legendary enough without him making a bigger arse of himself on top of it all. Hell, this might be the last time they saw each other. He didn't call out to her, but nor could he look away from her retreating form.

There was something in her hands, something she was stuffing back into a reticule... The letters. He was meant to post her letters, and hadn't had a chance to pick them up. Now he never would. His shoulders sank.

He hadn't just let her down. He had failed her completely.

Chapter Ten

A week later, Grace was back in the sea of spinsters. Now that the *beau monde* suspected her of being easy with her favors, the invitations had actually doubled. They just weren't to the sorts of places where one might find a marriageable suitor. She straightened her spine. This was the last of the upper-class soirées. She had to find a husband here. Tonight. Or she would never see her mother again.

She finally understood how desperation might drive weaker wills to strong drink. But all wasn't lost. Not yet. There were still a few hours left before dawn. She downed the last of her punch in one gulp. She had many, many faults, but giving up without a fight was not one of them. It was simply not an option. Even if the butler of tonight's crush almost hadn't let Grace and her maid through the door.

Where the dickens did that girl get off to, anyway? Grace peered through the crowd. Not that it signified. Her reputation was already suspect. She tore her gaze from the blank dance card hanging limply from her wrist and focused her eyes on the ballroom entrance in the hopes of espying a potential suitor. Any suitor.

But there were none. Grace lowered her eyes to her empty glass. No one rushed to refill her cup. No one noticed her at all.

At this point, she'd be grateful for one of the dirty old roués, as long as he didn't need her money and was willing to let her return to America for her mother. The rest of her list of requirements had gone out the proverbial window.

In a flurry, Miss Jane Downing rushed into the ballroom from an adjoining corridor, her eyes alight and her face flushed. Grace frowned. She couldn't recall Miss Downing ever moving at speeds greater than glacial, much less having color in her cheeks.

Beautiful and clever, Miss Downing was the one solid friendship Grace had managed to make since her arrival, and she was deeply sorry she wouldn't be able to keep it. Miss Downing was respectable. Grace was not. No matter what the girls might wish, society's rules were clear. And Grace would never ruin anyone she cared about by association.

To her surprise, Miss Downing practically wriggled when she caught Grace's eye. She made an inelegant beeline straight for the vacant seat at Grace's side. She threw herself onto the hard wooden chair as if it were a cool lake at the end of a hot race. Her slow, cunning smile was nothing short of victorious.

Grace narrowed her eyes. "What did you do?"

Miss Downing all but clapped her hands in glee. "You'll never guess! I was in the library, thumbing through the latest Radcliffe—forgive me, but I must know how a book ends before I know whether I can bear to read it from the beginning—when Lord Carlisle grabbed me by the hand and said, 'Jane—'"

"What?!" Grace's heart banged against her ribs. She had tried so hard not to even think about him these past few days, but just the sound of his name twisted her into knots all over again.

"Oh dear, you're not one of those the-end-of-the-book-is-sacrosanct snobs, are you? My brother Isaac about has fits every time he catches me reading the ending first, but I honestly cannot imagine—"

"Lord Carlisle grabbed you by the *hand*?" Grace's stomach soured. She was jealous of Miss Downing. Over a man she couldn't have. "He calls you *Jane*?"

"It *is* my name," Miss Downing responded primly.

It was all Grace could do not to grab her by the shoulders and shake her. Whatever news she'd come to impart, she was dragging it out a-purpose. But why? No matter. If Grace was angry and hurt and jealous, she would have to endure.

After all, she had no grounds to be displeased about whatever had just transpired in the library. No grounds at all for the bile in her throat at the thought of other women's fingers in the palm of Lord Carlisle's hand. Or for the blow to her chest at the realization that Lord Carlisle felt intimate enough to first-name Miss Downing in a private setting, when he wouldn't be able to pick Grace's given name out of a hat. Oh, stuff it all. Miss Downing *would* answer Grace's questions, or Grace would drown her in the ratafia bowl.

"How do you know him?" she demanded. "How does he know your name? Why did he grab your hand? Are you enamored of him?"

Grace's questions only served to stretch Miss Downing's smile even wider. Her grin faltered when she finally realized the depth of Grace's distress.

"Oh! Miss Halton, *no*. Not like that. Well, I mean, at one time, I had thought perhaps... Years ago, when Isaac took him to task for bending heads with me over a book, we discovered—to my utter humiliation—that

Lord Carlisle's interest in Sophocles' *Elektra* was not, in fact, feigned."

"Elektra?" Grace echoed blankly.

"None other. What had caught his eye wasn't the new feather in my bonnet or the lace fichu upon my bodice, but the uncut pages of a classical volume in original Greek text. I might have been a bookshelf for all the interest Lord Carlisle paid *me*."

Grace tilted her head. "You thought…"

"Only for a second." Miss Downing's sad smile brightened. "But now we are friends. Nothing like a blistering Isaac upbraiding to bond two hapless bibliophiles together, if only for one small moment in time. Besides, Isaac was right to be suspicious. If Lord Carlisle had but wished, I would happily have let him ravish me right there between Euripides and Aristophanes."

"*What*?" Grace choked on the word.

"Of course *you* couldn't understand. I imagine back home you must beat off the beaux with a broom. I don't have that problem. I'm shaped like a pear. The only thing I beat is dust from my bookshelves." Miss Downing's eyes darkened as she added fiercely, "I do not fear the Sword of Damocles. I *long* for it. But 'tis not the life I am given."

Grace toyed with her empty glass, suddenly uncomfortable. It was not fair for Miss Downing to judge herself lacking in comparison. Grace was no prize. She held up her wrist, displaying the empty dance card. "You're not the only one with a significant lack of suitors."

"Sure, *suitors*. You're quite infamous now that you drove an uncatchable man to fisticuffs in your honor, and while you quite correctly feel it has brought you all of the wrong kind of attention, I would trade places with you in a heartbeat."

Grace's sympathy turned to fury at Miss Downing's casual dismissal of the hell Grace lived in. "Rubbish. You offer to trade places without knowing the first thing about me, or why I am suffering through these balls to start with. I—"

"I have no clue why you're still in *this* ballroom. Not with the dashing Lord Carlisle awaiting you in the library. Impatiently, I am sure."

Her heart stopped. "He's what?"

"That was the rest of the story. Lord Carlisle grabbed me by the hand and said, 'Jane, please fetch Miss Halton here without delay. I'll be forever in your debt.' Imagine! An earl begging a bluestocking '*Please*'!" Miss Downing winked. "He must like you very much."

Grace stared back wordlessly. Her fingers trembled. Was this secret rendezvous in the library an attempt to avoid further damage to her reputation? Or was it something more? She twisted in her chair to scan the shadows. Where the devil did Peggy run off to this time?

"What are you looking for?"

"My maid. I have no idea where she is, but I can't leave the public eye without—"

"You can and you should. Perhaps you can win Lord Carlisle's love! I'd come along to chaperone you, but I have to wait for my brother." Miss Downing patted Grace on the hand. "Don't worry so much. It's a library. He's not the only one in there, anyway." She narrowed her eyes thoughtfully. "More's the pity, if you ask me. You might've had a chance for romance.

But you'd better make haste. Who knows how long he's willing to wait?"

Nodding, Grace pushed to her feet. And realized she still clutched her empty cup.

Miss Downing held out her hand with a sigh. "Give me your glass. It's fine. Everyone expects the plump girl to consume at least two of everything anyway. Now go take advantage of that delicious man before he discovers the complete set of Plato's *Dialogues* on the third bookshelf from the right and you lose his interest forever."

Chapter Eleven

Out in the main corridor, Grace realized she hadn't the foggiest idea where the library was even located. Miss Downing might have memorized every title on every shelf, but Grace had been so focused on finding a suitor that she'd never bothered venturing outside of any of the ballrooms or their attached gardens.

After several false starts and one whispered exchange with a hall boy, she was finally pointed in the right direction and closing fast on the correct room. She could only hope Lord Carlisle had not already left in frustration.

A thin strip of warm light flickered beneath the library door.

She turned the handle and stepped inside.

A stiff, mottled-purple wingback chair stood before the fireplace. An equally stiff, pallid-faced gentleman with glossy Hessians and glassy eyes sat upon the chair. Perhaps "sat" was the wrong word. It was more like he had been propped there.

Unmoving.

Despite the chill seeping through the windowpanes or the fire crackling at his feet, not a hair on the gentleman's head dared to ruffle, nor did any movement of his chest indicate he was still breathing. Were it not for the very occasional sluggish blink of his eyes, she could easily have imagined him lifeless, or carved of marble. Even now, he was little more animated than a corpse.

"Miss Halton?"

Lord Carlisle. She spun to face him.

He was even more beautiful than she remembered. Soft brown hair, curling above his ears and across his forehead. Golden brown eyes framed by dark, curling lashes. Wide lips, straight white teeth, a faint scent of mint on his breath.

Tonight, he had not been drinking. He smelled of lemon and soap and sandalwood. It made her want to step closer, to feel his muscles bunch beneath her palms as she stroked his arms. To push her fingers into his hair and open her mouth to his.

He was staring at her as if he could subsist on the sight of her alone. His lips curved, his eyes shining with promise. If the strange man weren't a few feet away, if she and Carlisle weren't in someone else's library, where anyone could walk in at any moment... Grace forced herself to tear her gaze from his parted lips, from the thought of what he might do with them.

What had Miss Downing said? *If Lord Carlisle had but wished, I would happily have let him ravish me right there between Euripides and Aristophanes.* Yes. Grace knew that feeling far too well. It took all her willpower to fight it.

"Why did you ask me here?" The words came out breathier than intended. She was furious with him—or should be, anyway—but the warmth in his eyes made her want to bury her face in his cravat and let him comfort her.

He took a step back. "Where the devil is your chaperone?"

Grace's smile was brittle. She'd have to let Miss Downing know that she wasn't the only one Lord Carlisle was immune to ravishing. It was fortunate she hadn't given in to her desire to throw herself into his arms. "My maid is attending to other matters."

"Nothing is more important than you or your reputation. I've done enough harm as it is, and I shan't compound it. Should we postpone our conversation?" He motioned toward the fire. "Xavier is harmless, but hardly a chaperone."

"Let's just be brief." Grace recalled Miss Downing's advice to seize the moment, but could not help sliding a doubtful glance toward the man in the wingback chair. He still hadn't moved. He might not even be breathing. "This is... Xavier?"

"Xavier, meet Miss Halton, the lovely young lady I've told you so much about. Miss Halton, meet Captain Xavier Grey. We have been the best of friends since we first escaped our leading strings, and recently served together in the King's army."

She took a longer look at Captain Grey. The impression of a marble statue did not lessen. Despite the fire, he emanated an eerie emptiness. Dark black hair. Stormy blue eyes. Lax features. He looked as though he'd drunk an entire bottle of laudanum. Or as if he simply had nothing left to live for.

Was Captain Grey grieving? Or was he no longer inside his head at all?

Her gaze flew back to Lord Carlisle. He rushed to take her hands, apparently misconstruing her concern over Captain Grey's mental state to be maidenly offense that the gentleman in question had not acknowledged the introduction.

"It's not that he's ignoring you," Lord Carlisle murmured in a voice so low Grace had to strain to hear him. "He hasn't spoken a word since before we were sent home. Please don't hold it against him. He's one of the best men I've ever had the privilege to know."

"I…" She let go of Lord Carlisle in order to step closer to the captain. His blank eyes showed no signs of recognizing their presence, no indication he realized he sat before a blazing fire in the sumptuous Seville library. "I'm very pleased to meet you, Captain Grey. I hope someday we might be friends."

No response. Not even a blink. She turned back to Lord Carlisle with a question on her face. He shook his head. Grace's heart ached for them both. That handsome, empty husk had once been Lord Carlisle's best friend. Though he might technically still be here, there was no doubt Carlisle knew he had lost him. But like Grace, Carlisle clearly was not one to give up easily.

He reached out for her, then shoved his hands behind his back.

Grace swallowed. She wished he had touched her, wished he had pulled her to him so they could hold each other tight. But it was good he had not. She might never have let go, and that was something she simply couldn't risk.

He cleared his throat. "Did you bring a letter for me to post?"

She smiled, surprised he had remembered. And very grateful.

"Many. I have a dozen letters. One for everyone I know." But she did not immediately pull them from her reticule. Touching them, handing them over, somehow made the questions written inside all the more real.

How is my mother? Am I too late? What if I can't bring the money home?

Grace's throat swelled tight and she swallowed hard. She must relinquish them. This might be her only chance.

Her shaking fingers dug the folded pages from her reticule. She pushed the missives into his gloved hands before she could lose her nerve. Did she still have any nerve left? Hot pinpricks stung the backs of her eyes and she blinked hard to clear them. The world was closing in on her from all sides, burying her alive in a world of glitter and silk. Had she wasted the last weeks of her mother's life, chasing an impossible dream? Was all this effort for nothing? Would she ever see her mother's grave, or was she stuck in England forever?

She fumbled with her reticule, trying to close the drawstring with her trembling hands. She was not too late to save her mother. She was *not*. But she needed to know for certain. Needed to know that when she got on that boat, her mother would still be waiting on the other side of the ocean.

Lord Carlisle tucked the bundle into a breast pocket. "I will frank these for you this very evening. I am sorry I was not able to do so the last time we met. I should never have leveled Mapleton before so many people, although he quite deserved it, and worse."

Grace set the reticule on the edge of a shelf before she dropped it. As apologies went, this one was... unexpectedly honest. He was not sorry to have struck the man that insulted her. He was sorry that his defense had brought more trouble than peace.

She motioned him to join her among the bookshelves for a little more privacy. The man before the fire might be silent, but she did not wish his eyes upon her when she asked Lord Carlisle her next question.

"You smelled of wine," she said quietly, her face as serious as her tone. "Were you drunk that night?"

The corner of his mouth quirked, but the smile did not reach his eyes. "Regrettably, no. Perhaps then I might have something to blame besides the flash of my own temper. When I overheard your name being spoken in such a manner… I'm afraid I reacted with my fist rather than my brain."

His fist, yes, but also his heart. He had been offended on her behalf, had wished to avenge her honor.

If only Society worked that way.

She took a deep breath. "When I smelled the alcohol on your breath, I…I'm afraid I may have overreacted."

He let out a bark of laughter. "I'm the one who got blood on my gloves. What the devil do you have to apologize for?"

"I'm not apologizing," she said quietly. "I'm explaining why I cannot bear to be around someone who drinks spirits."

His knuckle forced her chin up so her gaze met his. She shivered. His eyes had gone cold. "Did someone hurt you?"

"Irrevocably," she admitted, "but not the way you think. I was a baby at the time. Everything I know, I was told later. Back then, my mother was barely as old as I am now. My father was a physician, attending to a sick child in Bower Hill." She took a deep, shuddering breath. "Have you heard of the Whiskey Insurrection?"

Carlisle shook his head, his eyes dark. He had undoubtedly guessed how the tale would end. "Your father fought against the rebels?"

"My father was a healer. He was unarmed, save for his leather pouch of willow bark and cold compresses." Her voice wobbled. She forced herself to keep talking. "Ten army soldiers came to aid the house under siege, but by then almost six hundred armed rebels surrounded it. They wanted to kill General Neville. The general wasn't even inside."

Lord Carlisle pulled her into his embrace. "Never say they were at the wrong house."

"He was hiding in a ravine. It was the right house." She shuddered and closed her eyes tight. "It just had the wrong man inside."

"Six hundred to ten. It's not even a fight." Lord Carlisle's voice was hard, his body a rock. "There's no honor in slaughter."

"There was no honor at all," she said bitterly. "Only men and their whiskey."

He laid his cheek against her forehead and cradled her close. His heartbeat sped beneath her ear. "I'm so sorry, darling."

"After several hours, they let the women and children go." She swallowed the lump in her throat. "But not the men. Not my father."

"His patient?"

"Eight years old. Dead within a week. The rebels hadn't let the women and children take anything with them, for fear one might smuggle a weapon to use against them."

"The child's mother couldn't return for the medicine the next morning? After it was all over?"

"Return where? As soon as the women and children were gone, both sides opened fire. When the rebel leader fell, his troops set the house ablaze." She had seen the site, years later. She wished she hadn't. It was worse than a grave. "There was nothing left to come back to. Everyone was dead. Everything was ashes."

"All that destruction," he said slowly, then pressed his lips to her hair. "Just for some whiskey."

"Exactly." She shuddered and clung to him. "That's why I… If you…"

"I won't ever drink spirits around you again, and I promise to never drink to excess." His eyes burned into hers. "I swear it on this kiss."

Her mouth parted in surprise.

He lowered his head slowly, giving her time to pull away, the chance to reject him.

She could no more resist the allure of his mouth than the sea could resist the pull of the moon. She might end up leg-shackled to some dusty old roué, but she would go to her grave with the memory of this man seared into her soul. She, too, swore it. On this kiss.

His lips brushed hers. Light. Feathery. Still giving her a chance to say no, to turn away.

She would not. She would have this moment, every bit of this moment, because it would have to carry her through the rest of her life. This was *Oliver*. In her heart, he was hers. If only for this moment.

The next time his lips brushed hers, she suckled his lower lip into her mouth to taste him. She had dreamed of their lips, together. When he nipped at her lips, she eagerly opened her mouth to his.

His tongue swept inside, teasing gently. She gasped, grateful for the strong arms cradling her close. Her nipples tightened as if they could feel everything he was doing to her mouth just as clearly as if he were doing it to her naked breast. Swirling. Tasting. She swayed at the thought.

He suckled her lower lip into his mouth and she imagined he did the same to her nipples. How might it feel? Her nipples were taut against the thin linen of her sheath, the translucent silk of her dress. Her heart raced. Could he feel them through his waistcoat? She would die if he could, die if he could not. She wanted him to touch them, to ease the yearning ache building in her breasts and her belly and between her legs.

Gasping, she jerked her mouth from his before she gave into the temptation to have it all.

His mouth was only inches from hers, his breathing as irregular as her own. His smile was slow and full of sensual promise. "If you like, I can swear it on *two* kisses. If you're not convinced by the one, that is. I could probably even be talked into swearing on *three* kisses. Just this once."

She smacked his shoulder but didn't let him go.

"No? Are you sure?" He affected a very serious expression. "Promising is easy because I don't have any whiskey and I'm too poor to buy more. You're awfully fortunate I haven't a penny to my name. It's a blessing, really. Often I espy myself in a puddle of rain—I haven't a looking glass, you know—and I say to myself, 'Self, how dreadful it would be to actually have money. If you had the blunt, you'd waste it on foolish things, like a greenhouse full of jasmine for a certain young lady, or perhaps a thick woolen fichu for her gowns so less savory gentlemen are not tempted by the succulent curve of her breasts.'" He made a wolfish face in the direction of her bosom.

"Oh?" she asked breathlessly. The self-deprecation in his tone did nothing to lessen the romance of his words. Her heart turned over. If he presented her with a greenhouse full of flowers, she knew precisely how she'd help him christen it. She arched her back to lift her breasts higher. "I thought only foods could be succulent."

The teasing vanished from his eyes in a flash of passion and heat. She had no doubt then that he wanted her as fiercely and as completely as she wanted him. She could feel the heat of his flesh even through his clothes. "Definitely succulent. I absolutely, positively, would adore the opportunity to eat you."

"Eat... me?" she gasped. "But how?"

"I would start right here..."

The tip of his tongue traced the edge of her ear. Her breath caught at the sensation. She shivered. He nipped at the lobe, then touched his tongue to the soft sensitive skin just behind. She gripped his arms tighter.

"...and then I would continue here..."

His hot, sinful mouth pressed a series of exquisitely slow kisses from behind the lobe of her ear all the way down her throat, bit by bit, tasting and kissing until he reached the pulse point at the base.

Her entire body was on fire with the wanting of him. Every kiss to her neck, she felt on her breasts, on her stomach, between her legs. It was as if every inch of her body was attuned to everywhere his mouth touched. And yet she wanted more. She didn't want to imagine his fingers on her thighs or the promise of his mouth on her breast. She wanted to *feel* him. The hard muscle of his arms and powerful legs, the heat of his kisses against her bare flesh.

"...and then make my way down ever so slowly to here..."

The lace fichu was gone from her chest, snatched away as if by the wind. She leaned into him. Finally, finally, his tantalizing kisses came ever so slowly closer to where she wanted them most. She had forgotten to breathe, had forgotten everything about everything except for the feel of his lips on her skin and how much she wanted to lift her nipples to his open mouth and force him to suckle. And then she wanted to do the same, right back to him.

His lips pressed hot kisses from the base of her throat all the way down to the tops of her breasts, slowly enough to torture, hot enough to brand. His mouth closed over one of her straining nipples, his tongue rasping over the thin layers of silk and linen. She clutched his shoulders, his hair. She wouldn't let him up. Couldn't. He made her ache so deliciously, made her hurt and need and want.

He tugged down the edge of her shallow bodice. Breathless, she willed him to touch her. With a searing kiss, he covered her straining breast with his hand. She gasped as his fingers pinched the straining nipple. He was hers and she was his. She threw her head back as he bent his mouth to her naked breast and employed his talented fingers on the one yet hidden. Her thighs were damp at the sensation, her legs pressed tight as if to ease a pulsing need deep within. She wanted more. She wanted him to touch her, to feel her heat, her wetness. She—

The creak of hinges sounded a scant second before the library door flew open and two figures strode right into line of sight with Grace and Lord Carlisle.

"Oh dear," said Miss Downing with a startled look. "Are Isaac and I interrupting something?"

"Nonsense!" Grace dropped to the floor with one hand to her chest, feeling blindly for the fallen scrap of lace that was supposed to be covering her swollen bosom. "Just... You know. Euripides. I adore Greek playwrights."

Oliver was flush against the closest bookshelf, attempting to adjust his breeches without appearing to be doing so. He was failing miserably.

"Carlisle, is that you?" Mr. Downing stormed closer, hands on his hips. "What exactly is going on in here?"

"I believe Oliver was kissing Miss Halton just prior to your arrival," came a drowsy murmur from somewhere near the fire.

All four of them bent to stare at Captain Grey in astonishment.

"Xavier!" Oliver rushed to his side and gave him a fierce hug. "You're back!"

"And you've been kissing," Mr. Downing reminded him. "In the library!"

Oliver winced, and rubbed a hand over his face. "Honestly, Xavier? *This* is the moment you choose to awaken from a two-month fugue?"

Mr. Downing poked his finger at Oliver's chest. "The precise moment actually seems to be when your rakish mouth touched Miss Halton's innocent lips!"

"And her breast," Captain Grey mused drowsily. "Something about... 'succulent.'"

"Succulent breasts!" Miss Downing gasped.

Mr. Downing grabbed Grace's arm just as she finished shoving the lace fichu more or less back into place. "Miss Halton, this is very serious indeed. You have been well and truly compromised. Your reputation—"

"—will not suffer one whit," Oliver interrupted, his tone commanding and imperial. "I was overcome with passion because this lovely, virginal young lady has just agreed to be my wife."

"*What?*" Grace choked out in horror, her limbs draining of all feeling. His estate... Her *mother*...

Oliver elbowed her in the shoulder. "Act blissful, damn it. This time we *both* need rescuing. If you don't marry me, you'll never marry anyone, and I shall not abandon you to such a fate."

"It's true," Miss Downing stage-whispered. "You have to say yes. Captain Grey saw your breast."

Grace glared at her. "Nobody saw anything! We were behind that bookshelf and—"

"... something about 'eating' Miss Halton..." Captain Grey murmured. "I didn't quite catch..."

Oliver coughed and tossed a worried glance toward Grace. "I meant it... non-passionately?"

Mr. Downing's intractable gaze speared them both.

"Huzzah!" Grace managed with a bleak smile. "I'm to be married. There has never been a more blissful bride than I."

Oliver put his arm around her shoulders and cuddled her to him. "It is official. You have made me the happiest of men."

Awfully, she had the suspicion that he was at least somewhat telling the truth. He needed an heiress with significantly more money than she had to offer, but he didn't look like his heart had just been ripped from his chest and trampled to dust by a thousand horses.

Grace, on the other hand... It was finally over. Her last hopes, gone. Now there would never be any money to save her mother. She could not act happy. She could not even make eye contact, for fear of hot tears beginning to flow. As much as she liked Oliver, as much as she desired both his presence and his body, he was the worst possible match she could ever have made.

He needed her dowry even more than she did.

Chapter Twelve

Oliver stared into the face of the Black Prince.

For twenty-six years, the ghost of Edward the Black Prince had been both his nemesis and his brother. How Oliver had hated him, this dead young man with his bright yellow beard and rich blue mantle flowing rakishly from his royal shoulders. He had been both firstborn and favorite son to his father the king, and the only son who mattered to Oliver's father, the earl.

Yet he could not remove the painting from the wall. Hate it or not, it was as much a part of him as his own heart. The Black Prince was the only family he had left. His brother. His enemy.

Since the time he could read, Oliver had researched every scrap of history he could find about the man who held his father in thrall. As a young child, he'd hated the dead prince for all the things he could do that little Oliver could not—attend council meetings. Hold court. Lead battles. Marry for love. As Oliver grew older, he'd hated the dead prince for all the things he did that Oliver *would* not—massacre innocents. Burn and pillage.

All these years, he'd believed his father's disappointment in him stemmed from his inability to live up to the Black Prince's larger-than-life persona. But now, as he stood in his finely tailored clothes in the only corridor of the manor where paintings still adorned the walls, he was disquieted to realize how alike he and the Black Prince actually were.

Both were fearless. Foolish. And wrought destruction wherever they went.

Mirroring his hated cousin, Oliver had rushed into battle, inherited a title, attended the House of Lords. He'd pillaged his own bloody estate right down to the silver napkin rings. He was marrying a woman he could easily come to love. And while he did not massacre innocents, he left naught but misery in his wake.

He brought his fist to his forehead and closed his eyes. Poor Miss Halton. How she must despise him. She had made it abundantly clear that he was not the sort of husband she was looking for. Why would he be? Who could blame her? He was empty. As soulless and as useless as the cracked portrait upon this wall. All he saw again and again was the moment she realized he'd stolen her ability to choose her own future. They were to be married forthwith.

Her shattered expression would be scarred forever upon his heart.

He opened his eyes. The Black Prince gazed regally back at him. Fitting. Oliver did not deserve to have his portrait upon the wall. The Black Prince was a murderous, chivalrous, god-fearing contradiction, but he was well-loved by his father and his countrymen.

Oliver's gut clenched as he realized the truth with sudden clarity. *This* was why he'd joined the war, fought the front lines in battle. This was why he raced pell-mell into his ill-fated rescues. He just wanted to be useful for once in his life. To be needed. To be important to somebody—anybody—even if it were only one person. He wanted somebody to choose *him* for once. To want him. To love him.

But that was not his fate.

"My lord?" echoed a voice from down the corridor.

Oliver turned his back on the Black Prince and forced a smile for his butler. Ferguson would be leaving soon. Oliver had his letter of recommendation in his pocket. It was the least he could do. He was better than his father. He would not allow honorable people to slave for him when there was no money to pay their wages. Oliver could open his own doors, wash his own dishes.

"Yes, Ferguson?"

"There are visitors, my lord. I put them in the side parlor. I did not know where else to... Well. The sunlight is very pretty there."

Ah. Poor Ferguson. Someone finally paid a social call, and Oliver had left no furnished rooms in which to receive guests. "An excellent choice. The view of the garden is lovely from that angle. Who has come to call?"

Ferguson did not need to glance at the calling card in his hand. "Miss Halton and Mr. and Mrs. Mayer. Your bride and her grandparents are here."

Oliver's fingers went cold, even as a besotted thrill of excitement raced through his veins. His eyes ached for the sight of Miss Halton's smile. His heart dropped at what she must think of his bare walls, his empty parlor. How elderly were her grandparents? There was nowhere for them to sit, save the dining room. Perhaps he should move them in there. The great table and walnut chairs made the space look more, rather than less empty. Great swaths of space where the buffets had once been, faint rectangles where paintings had once hung. Sporadic candles instead of chandeliers.

This was no place for a bride. No prize for Miss Halton, who deserved so much more than he could give her.

He hoped they weren't staying for supper. Nervously, he ran a hand through his hair. *Shite*. He hoped they would leave and he hoped they would stay, because even as he was ashamed of his vast, vacant manor, the emptiness softened at the edges because Miss Halton was inside the walls. Her presence felt more like home than anything he'd ever felt in his life.

He hurried to the side parlor, slowing only when the open doorway was in sight. Three telltale shadows spilled across the floor.

She was here. His heart sped faster. She was *here*.

Chapter Thirteen

Oliver strode into the side parlor with his shoulders back and his head high. The estate might be a shadow of what it once was, but the manor was still standing and he remained its Black Prince.

He sketched a beautiful, courtly bow. "Mr. Mayer. Mrs. Mayer. Miss Halton. Welcome to my home."

The grandmother's moue of displeasure matched the sharp edge to her tone. She gestured at the bare walls with her walking stick. "This is a home? It's an embarrassment, is what it is. I've had better equipped stables. Do you realize one can see precisely where the furniture stood and the paintings hung? Don't expect me to return to this box. I will not. Mark my words."

"Grandmother, please," Miss Halton hissed as she dipped her respects. "You didn't curtsey."

"Nor shall I," Mrs. Mayer sniffed. "I'm not here to curtsey. I'm here to discuss your dowry. Look around you and tell me he doesn't prefer that we sign the contract as quickly as possible."

Eyes pained and cheeks flushed, Miss Halton flashed Oliver a pleading glance.

He smiled at her. He couldn't help it. Who cared if her grandmother was a rude old hag? She wasn't coming back; she'd said so herself. He honestly couldn't imagine a better wedding present than that.

"I see you smiling," Mrs. Mayer snapped. Despite her gray hair and the slight sag to her features, she was as brisk and spry as a woman half her age. Her quick, dark eyes took Oliver in with a glance. "I assume you compromised the chit specifically to get your hands on her money? Well, it's not her money. It's my money. And yet the girl is going to be yours."

Oliver could not wait to rid his bride of this horrible woman. And the grandfather—where was his pride? He neither supported his wife nor defended his granddaughter. Hands clasped behind his back, he gazed out the big picture window as if he wasn't paying the least attention at all. Perhaps he wasn't.

He could be deaf.

"Don't bother looking at Mr. Mayer for help," Mrs. Mayer barked sharply. "He'll sign when it's time. I'm accepting your suit not because you compromised the girl, but because of your title. The Mayers came from nothing and built our fortune from scratch. We have more money than most of you supposed aristocrats, and we're still nothing. Thus it gives me great pleasure to have a countess for a granddaughter. The snobs can take that and stuff it!"

Miss Halton—Grace—winced at her grandmother's vulgarity, but she had borne the brunt of snobbery firsthand. Oliver had long understood that it was his title and his father's money that gained him entrée into exclusive arenas.

"I will sign whenever you like," he said quietly. He peeled off his gloves to more easily handle the documents.

The important thing was not the contract. The important thing was Grace, and she was currently expiring of mortification. He hated to see her so miserable. If her grandmother hadn't excommunicated herself from their married lives, he would've happily done the job for her.

"I'm sure you'd sign your soul away for enough coin," Mrs. Mayer snapped. "Well, that's too bad. Earl or not—and compromise or not—you're not getting a penny more than I originally planned. I don't care how much pleasure it gives me to rub the 'countess' title into Society's face, it's a one-time purchase. After the wedding, you're on your own. Both of you. Is that quite clear?"

Oliver inclined his head. What did it matter what Grace's dowry amounted to? A thousand pounds was a mere drop in the bucket with an estate this size, but that wasn't why he was getting married. He was doing so because he *wished* to. He'd marry her if he had to put up the thousand pounds himself. He was going to make something of this earldom, make a good life for them both, if it killed him.

Which it just might. "Clear as crystal. Shall we summon our barristers or just have done and sign?"

Mrs. Mayer snatched the contract back from him. As she did so, her gray eyes widened slightly. She flipped his hand palm up, then grabbed the other one as well.

"Grandmother, what on *earth?*" Grace stepped forward as if to put her body between them.

Mrs. Mayer narrowed her eyes. "Do you see that? His hands are as ruined as a pauper's."

"Grandmother, stop it. He's an *earl*."

The older woman harrumphed. "Mr. Mayer is the decision maker around here. Mr. Mayer! Get over here and sign the contract."

"There's no table and no pen," he answered without turning from the window. "Have you a pot of ink in your reticule?"

So he wasn't deaf.

"Come to my office," Oliver suggested. "There's only one chair, but there's a desk, several plumes, and plenty of ink."

Nose held high, Mrs. Mayer preceded them out the parlor door as if the manor belonged to her.

Oliver took advantage of the opportunity to pull Grace into his arms and press a quick kiss to the top of her head.

"Lord Carlisle!" she whispered, eyes wide. "My grandfather!"

He glanced over his shoulder. Mr. Mayer was still facing the side garden, his back to the room. Oliver placed Grace's hand on his arm. "Mr. Mayer, if you'll follow us?"

As they traversed the corridors, he kept Grace firmly at his side. Partly to annoy her grandmother, but mostly because he loved the sensation of her warm fingers upon his arm and the scent of jasmine in her long black hair. He hadn't planned to wed—and she certainly hadn't wished to marry *him*—but he couldn't bring himself to regret it. She'd undoubtedly have been much better placed with any other toff in the ton, but no other man would dedicate the rest of his life to making her happy as Oliver fully intended to do.

She might not want him. She might never love him. But just once… he'd like to matter to someone.

He'd like to matter to *her*.

He gave her hand a quick squeeze as they entered the office, then turned to fetch plumes and ink as promised. He offered Mrs. Mayer his chair, but she waved it away.

"Mr. Mayer needs it more than I do. Go on and sit, you old fool. Lord knows your knees aren't what they used to be. Try not to break a hip getting over there."

Oliver watched as Mr. Mayer sank wearily into Oliver's leather chair.

These people might be horrid to Grace, were unquestionably not going to win awards for empathy and compassion, but on the other hand... they were *here*. In the same room. They *looked* at her. Spoke to her. Wished to meet her intended before giving their permission. Had offered to provide a dowry.

He could not like them, of course. Whether they cared for Grace or not, they had literally burned the lines of communication with her mother, and that was something he could not forgive.

Mrs. Mayer slapped the contract onto his desk.

Oliver took a closer look at the small print. One thousand pounds, to be deposited into his account the same morning as the wedding. Not a penny more, not a moment earlier. Marriage within two months time, or the contract is void.

Fine. He dipped his plume into the ink and signed. Mr. Mayer did the same.

Grace went very pale and very still, as if up until the moment of signing, a small part of her had expected angels to swoop in and brush the compromise away. Oliver's heart twisted. He was no angel. All he could do was try not to add to her worries.

Her voice wobbled as she asked, "Is there... Is there a dowager suite on the property?"

Mrs. Mayer snorted as if the idea were preposterous. "*I* will not be returning to his hovel, child. Make no great efforts on my account."

"I would visit," Mr. Mayer put in. "With a rifle. I think I saw pheasant behind the property."

Oliver ignored the interruptions. It was obvious whom Grace had meant. "Your mother?"

She nodded. "Perhaps she could make it. If we send enough money to cover doctors and medicine, and a companion to help her pack her bags—"

"What money?" Mrs. Mayer pursed her wrinkled lips. "You were caught with this paragon of society in the Seville family library during a soirée. You don't get prize money. You're fortunate you even get banns instead of a trip to the anvil."

Grace's mouth fell open. "Fortunate! You *have* to allow Mama time to get well enough to attend the wedding. She's my *mother*. And she's dreadfully ill. I don't even know—"

"I don't have to do anything," Mrs. Mayer said coldly. "I have *chosen* to donate one thousand pounds of my own money to the gentleman *you* chose to give liberties to. With what money are you going to send for your mother, child? You haven't a farthing, and Carlisle here has even less. This is it. The contract is signed. What'll it be, girl? A swift wedding, or a life of spinsterhood at home with your beloved grandparents? Don't you think you've already caused us enough trouble?"

Fury shone in Grace's pale green eyes, despite the blur of unshed tears. "It's no wonder my mother left home and never looked back. You're hateful."

"Left home?" Her grandmother snorted. "Tossed her out, is what we did. Much like you, she was too free with her favors. Why do you think you were born seven months after the wedding? I'm half surprised there *was* a wedding. I presume even in America, they know how to count."

Grace gripped the sides of her skirt, her knuckles white with anger. "You're saying... My father..."

"Was someone you never met. Not that it matters. You shan't repeat *all* of your mother's mistakes. I presume you're smart enough to avoid a seven-month baby, but just in case—you won't be leaving the house until the day of the wedding."

"But grandmother, I didn't— Lord Carlisle and I never—"

"That's what she said, too. Load of rubbish, wasn't it? That's why I've already reserved the church for your wedding. The date is set."

"I'm not my mother! You can't punish me for something she may or may not have done twenty-two years ago. She forgave you. Why can't you forgive her?"

"She never asked me to," her grandmother replied bitterly. "I'm her mother. That's all it would have taken."

"Liar." Grace's voice was cold. "Forgiveness is something that happens in your heart. An organ I doubt you possess."

Oliver pulled her into his arms, holding her from behind. Her shoulders remained stiff and unyielding.

"Don't be nice to me," she muttered, twisting free from his arms. "Don't you dare be sweet and sympathetic or I won't be able to keep the tears from falling. She doesn't deserve to see me cry."

He let her go.

She was right. Her grandparents didn't deserve her tears, or her smiles, or any part of her. They didn't deserve Grace at all. He was glad her mother had run off to America. Her father sounded like a wonderful, kindhearted man, no matter the biology of their relationship. And her mother was a saint. Imagine, growing up under the same roof as this dour-faced dragon, and still managing to raise a daughter as extraordinary as Grace.

"See you at the wedding?" he asked softly. He would wait years, if she wanted. Dowry be damned.

When she glanced up at him, her eyes had dried but her voice was hollow. "I'll be the girl in the veil."

He nodded. "I'll bring the flowers."

Her crooked smile broke his heart.

When she walked out the door, she took a piece of his soul with her.

In dismay, he realized that the fate worse than marrying someone he didn't like might be marrying someone he did.

Chapter Fourteen

After Ferguson had secured the latch and the sound of carriage wheels faded into nothing, Oliver called all his servants into his office. When his father was alive, no more than a dozen people might've wedged themselves in amongst the chairs and cabinets and rolling secretaries. Now it was only Oliver, and a single desk. They could've danced the minuet with room to spare, if they'd been of a mind to.

Of course, no one felt like dancing. Oliver was about to do one of the hardest things he'd ever done in his life, and his trusting, hardworking staff... Well, who knew where they'd be tomorrow. All he could hope is that they found somewhere better than here.

He rose to his feet. He would hold his head high and meet everyone's eyes. He would not strip them of their dignity.

"Ladies and gentlemen," he began. His voice was low, but steady.

No one moved. All eyes were fixed on his.

"It has recently come to my attention that my father—God rest his soul—left the earldom in a state of arrears. You no doubt noticed when your wages were no longer forthcoming, and you all helped when I was forced to take action to repay those debts." He waved a hand toward an empty wall where three perfect rectangles indicated where a triptych of oil paintings had once hung. "The unfortunate consequence is that the maids now have less surface area to dust."

The smiles were quick, but nervous. No one laughs while awaiting the axe to fall.

He picked up the stack of sealed notes on his desk and began to call out names. "Ferguson... John Coachman... Millie..."

"What is this, my lord?" asked his valet when it was his turn to pick up his document. He held it by the very edge, as if it were poisonous to the touch. "Are you sacking us all?"

Oliver shook his head. "Not exactly. I'm giving you all your freedom. Freedom to do whatever it is that's right for you. All of you are now in possession of a glowing, personalized letter of recommendation. You are absolved of the need to give notice. You may leave right now, or at any time in the future. It is my hope that with these letters, each of you can easily find employers who deserve you."

His cook's round cheeks flushed. "We're no longer welcome here?"

"You are *always* welcome here," Oliver said fiercely. "This is your home as much as mine. You are the only family I have ever had. It is because I love you all that I am giving you the means to leave. There are no chairs to sit on and barely enough wood for the fire. I will have a wife in a few weeks' time and I don't know how I'll even feed her, much less find money for your wages. I'm doing my best to invest wisely, to improve efficiency, but it may not bear fruit for another year at least. How can I ask you to stay on, in conditions such as those?"

"You don't have to ask us," said Ferguson, his voice gentle. "You said it yourself. We're a family."

The cook stared at Oliver in bewilderment. "I could no more leave you to starve than I could starve my own children. I cooked for you and your father before you, and if the Lord grants me enough life to do it, I intend to cook for your sons, too."

His valet shook his head as if the very idea was preposterous. "Why do you think we stayed on, when it was clear your father couldn't pay us? It wasn't for him, my lord. We stayed because of you."

Oliver's throat tightened. They'd stayed for *him*. He now knew exactly what Grace had meant about the danger of kind words when one is desperately trying to hold one's feelings inside. As he stared at the sea of earnest faces, his head spun in wonder. No matter how many times it had felt that way, he had never been alone.

"Thank you," he said gruffly. "I... thank all of you."

Millie the upstairs maid flashed him a saucy grin. "We love you too, my lord."

Before he could respond, she and the other giggling chambermaids were out the door and gone.

As all of his servants made their bows or dipped their curtseys, Oliver felt each one as though it were an embrace. He'd gone through his entire childhood without once being hugged, or ever feeling like his home was a sanctuary. For the first time in his life, it was.

When the last of his staff had taken their leave, he made his way from his office to the Hall of Portraits. This time when he gazed up at the Black Prince, it was not with hate or with envy, but with a sense of finality. The Prince was family as much as anyone... But he

could do the most good by saying good-bye. Oliver had
servants to feed. Debts to pay. A bride to cherish.

What was one more empty rectangle on the manor
wall?

Chapter Fifteen

Grace balled up her latest letter and hurled it into the fire. What was the point of writing letters? Her grandparents refused to post them and she had no means or money of her own. Even if she did, the wedding was less than a week away. By the time her note arrived, the ceremony would already be over.

She couldn't even give her correspondence to Lord Carlisle to post anymore. Her grandparents hadn't let her leave their sight from the moment the contract was signed. Not that she could run into him casually, even if she could leave the house. According to the scandal sheets, he hadn't been seen in weeks. Grace lowered her forehead to her writing table and sighed.

Was that her fault, too? That he was no longer attending events? Or had he simply run out of money? She could easily imagine him giving up all comforts and diversions in order to save his pennies for once they were married.

Her chin sank to her chest. At times like these, she missed her mother so sharply and so completely that it felt like her heart was empty and the yearning endless. Her mother would hug her and tell her she loved her, and hold her tight. But Mama wasn't here. Grace didn't even know if she was still alive. The first chance she'd get to sail back to America wouldn't be for another week. Not until the day after the wedding.

She closed her eyes. Oh, Oliver. Her heart ached at what she was about to put him through. She didn't want to leave him. She could say it was for his own good, that he'd be better off without another mouth to feed or a dependent to look after, but she'd seen the warmth in his eyes when he kissed her forehead in his empty parlor. He might regret having been compromised, but he wasn't sorry it had been with *her*.

Heaven knew it was mutual. How she wished things could have worked out differently! Her nerves sizzled with frustration. Since her grandparents refused to send aid to her mother, she had no choice but to leave immediately after the wedding. It wouldn't be his fault if she didn't reach her mother before it was too late, but she would still be resentful for the rest of her life. She couldn't put any of them through that. Her hands twitched as she rocked back in her chair.

She rubbed the back of her neck, squeezing harder than necessary. There was no right answer. She would go home, and if her mother were healthy enough, she would bring her right back. And if Mama was too sick or Grace was too late... well, the money would be spent either way. She'd spend the last ha' penny on medicine and surgeons if need be. If that didn't work, there'd be grave to dig and a stone to buy and a "year" of mourning that would never truly end...

No. She leapt to her feet. She couldn't think that way. Her hands were tied until after the ceremony, but she'd be on the first boat out the morning after. Until then, she had to keep calm, keep breathing. It was just one more week. Less! Just six interminable days remained. Then she'd have Carlisle for a blissful, whirlwind twenty-four hours. She was determined to savor every moment of her wedding day. Their wedding night.

Because the next morning, she'd be on a boat. The thought filled her with as much regret as it did relief. But what choice did she have? Carlisle would understand the need to rescue her mother. He *had* to. It would break her heart if he did not.

She washed the ink from her fingers and then made her way to the stairs. Below, all was quiet. Her grandparents had made noises about paying a call upon a neighbor. If Grace was lucky, that would give her a few minutes to curl up on one of the plush silk sofas without them breathing over her shoulder. She tiptoed down the stairs. No one crossed her path.

Her grandparents' mansion was even larger than Carlisle's, and opulent to the point of ostentatious. Every corner boasted heavy marble busts. Every edge that could be gilded, was.

She wouldn't miss the gaudy extravagance, but she would miss easy access to the newest fashion plates, and a comfortable chaise longue upon which to enjoy them. Even Carlisle's estate would seem positively luxurious compared to the claustrophobic shared cabins upon the ocean vessel, where the stink of too many people clogged one's nose and the relentless pitching of the sea emptied one's stomach. Her belly turned at the unpleasant memory.

Her jaw set. She would survive the upcoming voyage.

Book in hand, Grace hurried toward her favorite sitting room—and pulled up short inside the doorway.

There, reclining upon the very chaise longue she'd been looking forward to using, was her grandmother. The pelisse about her shoulders and dry boots upon her feet indicated they had not yet made it to the neighbor's house, but would be leaving shortly. Her grandfather, similarly attired, sat in the wingback chair closer to the fireplace. He looked up first, but did not smile. Nobody in this house smiled.

"Well, here's Grace." He stretched his back. "We can let her read this one, can't we?"

Only then did Grandmother Mayer raise her gray head from the letter she'd been reading. The look she shot her husband could have boiled iron. She shoved the folded parchment in Grace's direction as if her very presence had soured its contents.

"Read it, then. It's for you."

Mama! Grace's heart leaped. Her entire body was so infused with joy that she couldn't even bring herself to be angry at her grandparents for breaking the seal and reading it first. They were finally letting her hear from her mother! Nothing else mattered.

The book fell from her fingers as she swooped forward to save the letter before her grandmother changed her mind and tossed it into the fire with the rest of the undelivered correspondence. Hands shaking as much from fear as excitement, Grace unfolded the ivory page and read the first line:

My future countess,

Pain ripped through Grace's heart, followed by an all-encompassing emptiness. Of course it was not from her mother. If there had been, it was ashes by now. This letter, too, would have shared the same fate, had she not entered the parlor at this precise moment. There would be no word of her mother's health or lack thereof until

Grace stepped onto Pennsylvania soil. Until then, all she had were her hateful grandparents.

And Oliver. She had Oliver. Her savior and her curse.

Swallowing the lump of despair in her throat, she turned back to the letter.

My future countess,

Forgive me that I no longer think of you as Miss Halton, but rather as Lady Carlisle, mistress of both my estate and my heart. I know that you do not love me and would not have chosen our union, and to that all I can do is everything within my power to be the sort of husband a wife can trust, respect, and perhaps come to care for.

To that end, I am writing to inform you that I have taken the liberty of opening an account in your name at the Bank of England on Threadneedle Street. This is the same branch in which I manage my own finances, and therefore holds the account that will receive your dowry the morning of our wedding. As soon as the funds arrive, they will be debited from my account and deposited into yours. To withdraw any amount of your choosing, you have only to present yourself at the bank and ask for it. This account is not in my name. The money is yours.

As you have no doubt ascertained, I lack sufficient resources to spoil you as extravagantly as I wish. However, I am able to grant the one desire that you *wish—for these funds to be used to aid your mother as you see fit.*

I do not labor under the misapprehension that this gesture should be construed as a wedding

present, nor do I seek gratitude for having
undertaken these steps. I cannot gift to anyone what
was never mine to begin with. The money has
always been yours. I am simply giving it back.
     Faithfully yours,
     Oliver

Grace closed the letter with shaking fingers. Her
eyes stung. That beautiful, selfless, idiotic man. Giving
her the freedom to walk away and leave him! Of course
she would not spend the entirety at once while he toiled
to save the earldom from ruin. She would withdraw just
enough money to reach Pennsylvania and provide for
her mother. The rest was his. *He* was the one who
deserved it.

"I must respond at once. Can you please see that
Lord Carlisle receives—"

"No." Her grandmother's cold voice was flat with
finality. "You will see him at the church, and that is
soon enough."

"But he—"

"I read it. He is a perfect fool, but that is his
decision. He can do with the money—and with you—as
he wishes. But not before the wedding. There will be no
more letters between now and then. No contact of any
kind. I will not have another scandal under my roof."

"How is a letter possibly scandalous? You can even
read it before you post it. I swear there won't be—"

"Not until the wedding."

Grace's fingers curled. They were so awful, so
unfair. Because their daughter had defied them twenty-
two years earlier, Grace could not be trusted with
parchment and ink?

Heart thudding dangerously, she turned from her grandparents and stalked out of the parlor.

"Where are you going?" her grandmother's imperious voice demanded from within the sitting room. "I'll lock you in your chamber if you force me to, young lady. I won't have scandal brought upon this house again."

Grace didn't answer. She couldn't, not without screaming. Her pulse pounded in her ears. She needed fresh air. She needed to *escape*. Hands shaking, she fled through her gilded prison and out the front door, anger inuring her to the sharp bite of the winter wind. She had to speak to Carlisle. To explain—

The carriage! It was at the ready, waiting to take her grandparents to call upon their neighbors.

She sped across the frozen lawn and up into the coach's black interior before the tiger could leap down and help her in, before good sense could change her mind.

"Carlisle Manor," she ordered the driver. "Hurry!"

The horses were immediately in motion, their hooves crunching the grass and then racing across the gravel stones to the gray dirt road.

Grace blinked in surprise. She twisted against the squab to peer through the window, her heart beating faster than ever. There was only the briefest glimpse of the manor entrance before the red brick wall lining the property blocked it from view. Already they were on the main road, out of earshot and out of sight.

She turned back to the front of the carriage. Why on earth had the coachman obeyed her? He'd been awaiting her grandparents, not some half-wild chit without even enough sense to don a pelisse and some sensible shoes. Except... he *couldn't* question her, she realized with sudden clarity. Not when he was a servant and she was not.

If he'd been previously instructed not to heed her commands, that would've been one thing. But of course her grandmother had never supposed Grace would ever be in a position where she might give commands. She hoped the old bat wouldn't take it out on the poor coachman. Mentally, Grace deducted a little more from her dowry in the coachman's name, just in case.

Shivering, she bent to pick up the woolen blankets lying folded on the carriage floor and discovered red-hot warming bricks beneath. She shook her head. Of course her grandparents would have every convenience at their disposal, even for a five-minute jaunt to a neighboring property.

Steam filled the carriage as she pulled off her snow-dusted slippers and placed them atop one of the bricks. The other brick she kept between her feet. She draped one of the blankets over her shoulders, but after a few minutes let it drop. Between the hot bricks and her layers and long sleeves, the carriage was almost too warm. The image of her grandfather wearing his coat as he sat before the fire popped into her mind and she smiled despite herself. The bricks were likely his idea. She would thank him for it later.

Right before they manacled her to the attic wall.

She had no illusions about the remaining days before the wedding. Once she returned to her grandparents' home, they would never let her leave the house again. This was her one chance to speak to Carlisle before the deed was done. She had to make it count.

When the coachman pulled up at Carlisle Manor, she all but flew out of the carriage and to the front door.

The butler opened the door almost as quickly as she released the knocker.

"Miss Halton!" Surprise colored his face, but he immediately motioned her in. "I'm afraid you've just missed Lord Carlisle. If you're willing to wait perhaps an hour or two, he's sure to be back quickly."

She rubbed her temples. An hour was much too long. By now, her grandparents had one of their many other coaches readied and stocked with warming bricks, and were on their way here. After all, where else was she likely to go?

"Do you... Can you tell me where he went? If it's not breaking a confidence?"

"Of course." The butler seemed more surprised by this question than the fact of her unexpected presence on the doorstep in the first place. "You are our mistress now. Lord Carlisle already informed us that your word is to carry the same weight as his. I have no doubt he would wish for you to find him, if that is your desire."

"It is my deepest desire," she said fervently and motioned to her coachman to join them, so that he might overhear any pertinent directions. "Where is he?"

"At the pawnbroker on Fleet Street, near the Old Bailey." The butler turned to her driver. "Do you know the place?"

The coachman nodded. "Of course."

The man was far too well trained to give any hint of the astonishment he must certainly feel at the progressively stranger turns of events. He simply helped Grace back into the carriage and set off for downtown London.

The bricks had lost their warmth by the time the carriage clopped past St. Paul's churchyard and came to rest before an unassuming facade. This time, she allowed the tiger to hand her down with considerably more decorum than she'd shown at Carlisle Manor.

Tiny bells tinkled overhead as she pushed open the door to the pawnbroker's shop and stepped inside. To her surprise, the coachman leapt from the carriage to join her.

When she glanced at him, he murmured, "A lady does not visit a pawnbroker, miss, and certainly not by herself."

She nodded, reminded once again of all she didn't know about England. There were rules back home, of course, about what a lady did and didn't do. But Grace had never been a lady, and her small farming town was the sort of place where anyone can and did go everywhere, without fear of bodily harm or damage to one's reputation. She had so much to learn before she could become a wife Carlisle wouldn't be ashamed of, much less a countess to be proud of.

"May I help you, miss?"

Grace whirled to face the pawnbroker. "I hope so. That is, I'm looking for Lord Carlisle. I was told he might be here?"

"Your information is accurate but your timing, I'm afraid, is just a few moments off. He left not ten minutes ago."

She had missed him. Her shoulders slumped. Now what? She couldn't go back to Carlisle Manor. By now her grandparents had stationed armed guards there, primed to abduct her upon sight. She could write a letter, at least, and have the pawnbroker post it...

Impossible. She covered her face with her hands at the irony. Without her dowry, she hadn't tuppence to her name, much less enough coin to purchase writing implements on top of it. She certainly hadn't thought to bring paper and an inkpot with her, and a pawnbroker was the last sort of person who would offer his own for free.

She wondered what Oliver might have brought here and then flinched to realize the answer was probably: everything. The shop was stuffed floor to ceiling with crates and boxes and locked shelves brimming with every sort of object. Every pawnbroker in the city likely contained a good percentage of Carlisle Manor's treasures.

She crossed her arms over her chest and rubbed warmth back into her upper arms. Half-witted to be out in this cold without a pelisse. At least her day dresses were warmer than her eveningwear. Those were light and flimsy to combat the heat of so many people and so much dancing, but were likely the least sensible thing to wear outside of a ballroom. Expensive silks were hardly proper defense against the bitter London chill, or the—

Expensive silks. Oh, if *only* she were wearing any one of her ridiculous evening gowns! Her shoulders caved. It wouldn't matter. There were no dresses displayed upon the walls. This was the sort of place one sold antiquities and jewels, not silk-and-lace trousseaus.

She cast her gaze about the shop in despair. Useless. Worse than useless. She couldn't even buy Oliver a wedding present. The man deserved *something*. After all, she was leaving him with nothing. Slightly richer, yes, but without a wife. She couldn't come back without her mother, and she couldn't put Mama on one of those horrid boats until her health was back. She would nurse her back to health, even if it took years.

And Oliver? A missing wife was worse than a dead one—he wouldn't even be able to remarry if she didn't come back. Not for money, and not for love.

It wasn't about him forgiving her for abandoning him, she realized dully. If she couldn't make it back, she might never forgive herself.

"Is there anything here that catches your eye?" The pawnbroker gestured toward a locked glass case with earbobs and other baubles inside.

"What happens to these things?" she asked instead. "People give you their treasures and you sell them to others?"

"Nobody *gives* me anything. Everyone walks out of my shop with more money in their pockets than when they came in." The pawnbroker puffed out his chest. "But to answer your question, it depends. Many of my customers avail themselves of my services. I hold a given item for a specified amount of time. If they return my capital and its agreed-upon interest, I return their object and the promissory note."

She tapped her chin and nodded.

"Other customers do not want their objects back. They prefer a small increase in money. In those cases, yes, I am free to resell those items at the time and at the price of my choosing. For example, Monday next I've an auction scheduled for a painting that's recently come in, free of vowels." He gestured toward a back room and chuckled. "I expect a portrait of the Black Prince to net a princely sum, indeed."

Grace's fingers went cold. He couldn't have such a painting in his possession. Oliver would *never* part with the Black Prince. Everyone knew—

Oh, no. She thought of the note he had written her. He was too proud, too kindhearted to accept the dowry money he needed so badly, and so he had sold the only thing of value he had left. Romantic fool. It was her fault he had given up a family heirloom. He'd never get it back, not if it was meant to be auctioned on Monday because he hadn't secured a promissory note...

"May I see it?"

"Of course."

The pawnbroker led her and the coachman to a side room, where a stunning portrait hung four feet tall on the wall. The paint was cracked with age in some places, but larger than life and full of color. Oliver's brown hair was much darker than the Black Prince's yellow locks, but his muscular shoulders and regal bearing matched down to the brushstroke.

Cousins, someone had told her. No one could doubt it. She couldn't let it be sold to someone else. Not when Oliver thought of the Black Prince as family.

"How much do you think you will get for it?"

The pawnbroker leaned forward, eyes bright with interest. "Would you like to put in a bid for it?"

"I must bid? Are you saying the painting cannot be sold outright?"

He laughed and shook his head. "Why would I sell it outright when I can make far more money at auction?"

"How much?" she repeated. "What does an old painting go for? Fifty pounds? One hundred?"

He grinned. "Any old painting, perhaps. But not a portrait of the Black Prince. It's worth seven or eight hundred pounds on its own merit, but at auction... The family history alone will fetch a few hundred more."

Over a thousand pounds. She slumped into the coachman. Even if she handed over every penny of her dowry, it still wouldn't be enough.

"Do you take evening gowns?"

The pawnbroker's head jerked up, startled. "What?"

"Dresses made of the finest fabrics, by the most famous of the London modistes."

"No. I don't think anyone—"

"They're dreadfully expensive," she insisted. "I even have some new ones that have never been worn. They can be let out, tucked in... Any lady would snap up the opportunity to have even one of these at a fraction of the original cost."

His lips hinted at a smile. "How many of these dreadfully expensive gowns do you have?"

"Dozens. I'll sell you all of them in exchange for the Black Prince."

He laughed. "I doubt their value will even come close. Feel free to bring them by, however. I never turn down a client without seeing what he has to offer."

Grace inclined her head, her palms sweaty. If it still weren't enough to buy back the Black Prince, perhaps her dresses would at least finance a return voyage to America to care for her mother. Then she could return her dowry money to Oliver. It wasn't ideal, but at least she would not be leaving him with less than what he started. If what he preferred was his wife... Well.

She couldn't have all her wishes granted either.

Chapter Sixteen

Three weeks later, Oliver stood at the altar awaiting his bride and valiantly tried not to fidget. He'd never been so nervous in his life. Every part of him was on edge, every nerve twitching with anticipation. It was as if he'd stepped onto a battlefield, not into a church.

His body thrummed with energy. With the wrenching desire to make this day perfect, and the bitter knowledge that he could not. His bride deserved so much. Yet this was all he had.

Weddings were typically small affairs with family and a few close friends. In this instance, the ceremony was considerably smaller.

The very presence of his four best friends showed how deeply they cared for him. Xavier, still withdrawn, but moving of his own accord. Bart, out in public for the first time since he'd been fitted with the false leg. Sarah Fairfax, huge belly and all. Even Ravenwood was there, a sappy grin overtaking his arrogant countenance. For a sobersides, the man loved weddings.

Oliver was happy to oblige. He just wished he could give Grace more than this.

Four people. Total.

No family present for the bride or the groom.

In Oliver's case, he *had* no family. In Grace's case... Well, he'd tried. Harder than he'd believed humanly possible. Yet even her grandparents hadn't bothered to make an appearance at the church they'd reserved.

He'd signed the contract. He supposed that truly was all they cared about. In which case — good riddance to bad relatives. Grace might've agreed to be his bride only because her circumstances had forced her, but Oliver had not. He fully intended to prove that his love for her was the one and only reason he was standing at the altar.

Just as soon as she arrived. He slipped the fob from his pocket to check his watch. Well after nine. He lifted his fingers to his neck to adjust his cravat then immediately forced his hands down at his sides. If he touched his cravat one more time it would hang from his throat like a limp white nappy. But why hadn't they started? Where the devil was his bride? And the priest? His cravat was much too tight. He was suffocating from all this linen. From this cavernous, empty cathedral.

He rolled back his shoulders and tried to laugh it off. Ha, ha, ha. He'd been standing there for half an hour or more. Grace would never jilt him at the altar... would she? He glanced at his friends but couldn't hold their gazes for long. Not when Grace still wasn't here. It would be a right popper of a jilting if she'd had the foresight to cancel the priest but failed to inform the groom.

Just when he was checking the hour for the twentieth time in as many seconds, the door swung open and Grace entered the church. Oliver's heart stopped at the sight of her, then sped twice as fast as before. She was more beautiful than he'd dreamed possible.

She wore no veil, but Oliver preferred it that way. He didn't want anything between them, not even a thin piece of semi-transparent netting. He loved to gaze upon her, to watch those incredible light green eyes twinkle. He hoped they'd twinkle, at least. Whenever they did, the rest of the world disappeared. She wasn't smiling, but then he wasn't smiling either, was he, with his stomach all tied up in knots like this. Except yes, yes he was smiling, he was giddy beyond all measure to see her (finally) here, walking toward him.

The gown she was wearing was a soft, shimmering lavender. Utterly perfect, really. He nodded at Miss Fairfax, who recognized her cue and lumbered to her feet at once. Bless Sarah, with her big belly and bigger heart. She'd wanted to do something special for Grace, make her some sort of crown of flowers like she'd seen in fashion plates, and Oliver had shocked her speechless by having an opinion on which flowers to use.

Miss Fairfax arranged the halo of jasmine atop his bride's head.

With the delicate flowers encircling her long black hair, Grace looked more like a fairy princess than a countess. He wished he could say she also looked radiant, but the truth was his bride was a touch gray.

Then the priest came bustling in, somehow managing both to hurry and to seem stately, in that commanding way that priests often have. He took Grace's elbow and led her to the left side of the altar before taking his place just behind.

Oliver grinned. He couldn't help himself. She was wearing his flowers and she was close enough to touch. He could practically kiss her from this distance if he wished to. And did he ever wish to. He wouldn't embarrass her, of course. This was not the moment for kisses.

She didn't love him right now, of course she could not. Nor should she. At the moment, he was nothing. A man with a failing earldom, a chimera with an empty house.

It was not what anyone wanted, not her, not him. But he could become what she wanted. He would make the Carlisle estate the strongest earldom in England even if it meant no sleep for the next ten years. He would marry her again if she liked, have a thousand wedding breakfasts, a ceremony to rival a king's. Anything she wished, he would ensure that she possessed.

"Dearly beloved," said the priest.

Oliver's heart stopped. Again. He reached for Grace's hands, then just as quickly dropped them. It wasn't the moment yet to join hands. Soon. The ceremony was finally beginning. A shiver raced along his spine. They were almost married.

"We are gathered here in the sight of God and in the face of this congregation"—here the priest cast a baleful eye at the motley foursome bearing witness—"to join together this man and this woman in holy matrimony."

Oliver stopped listening. Not a-purpose, of course; these were the most important words of his life. His ears had stopped listening all on their own. His senses had simply shut down to everything that wasn't Grace. All he could smell was the sweet scent of her hair. All he could see was her lovely pale face, her eyes so large and green, her eyelashes coal black. He was consumed with the desire to taste her, to have her. To hold her close. This was the woman he was marrying. Grace was finally going to be his.

"I require and charge you both," said the priest, his voice like flames upon Oliver's skin, "as ye will answer at the dreadful day of judgment when the secrets of all hearts shall be disclosed, that if either of you know any impediment why ye may not be lawfully joined together in matrimony, ye do now confess it."

Oliver fought a nervous chuckle at the idea. Any reason like what, that the bride didn't truly wish to marry him? This time he did grab her hands, proper timing be damned. His fingers wouldn't tremble so with her hands in his. For her, he had to be strong. For her, he would do anything.

"Oliver York, Lord Carlisle," the priest thundered.

Oliver's throat went dry as dust, his tongue suddenly ten sizes too large. This was it. This was when they pledged themselves to each other.

"Wilt thou have this woman to be thy wedded wife, to live together after God's ordinance in the holy estate of matrimony? Wilt thou love her, comfort her, honor and keep her in sickness and in health, and forsaking all others, keep thee only unto her, so long as ye both shall live?"

Oliver smiled. The answer must be in his eyes, for it was already in his heart. "I will."

The priest turned to address the bride. "Miss Grace Halton."

Grace flashed Oliver a tentative smile. Her eyes were huge as she stared up at him.

"Wilt thou have this man to be thy wedded husband, to live together after God's ordinance in the holy estate of matrimony? Wilt thou obey him, and serve him, love honor and keep him in sickness and in health, and forsaking all others, keep thee only unto him, so long as ye both shall live?"

138   Erica Ridley

The ensuing silence was so complete and so terror-
inducing that one could've heard a pin drop. In fact,
Miss Fairfax's reticule fell from her hands, spilling half
the pins of England upon the wooden floor, and nobody
so much as noticed. They were all leaning forward,
clutching each other's arms, looking just as concerned
as Oliver was starting to feel.

If by "concerned," one inferred a complete and utter
terror that one's bride was going to say *no* right in front
of everyone, and he was going to lose his chance for
love.

"I will," Grace whispered, her eyes shimmering.

Were those tears? Oliver was probably holding her
hands too tightly. Oh God, he'd been gripping her in
mortal fear. He relaxed his fingers. What if she'd meant
to say no, and he quite literally hadn't let her get away?
So be it. She wasn't going anywhere, his countess. He
would not let her. Not now.

The priest glanced up from the altar. "Who giveth
this woman to be married to this man?"

Shite. Oliver's heart sank as he watched his bride's
dull eyes search the meager audience. There was no one
to find. His hands grew clammy. For once, he would
have been glad for the Mayers' presence. Grace's
expression was stricken.

Had she not noticed until this instant that her
grandparents were not there? And of course the most
important person of all was also absent. She was getting
married without her mother.

Poor Grace. He knew how much she'd wanted her
mother to be there on her wedding day. She'd probably
dreamed of it her entire life, taken it for granted that of
course her mother would be at her side. And now here
she was, halfway across the globe, marrying a man

who'd compromised her in a library of all places, and there wasn't one single person present to stand up on her behalf.

"I will."

Oliver's head jerked up to see Ravenwood rise to his ducal feet, tall and dark and arrogant, making it look for all the world as though of *course* he was giving away Miss Halton, they'd planned it all along, things were marching precisely as they ought. Thank God for Ravenwood. He reached her side with both speed and grace, somehow seeming to give comfort to the bride whilst lending pomp and dignity to the ceremony.

The priest nodded as if dukes gave away American misses all the time during conspicuously sudden wedding ceremonies. He pried Oliver's hands from Grace's and rearranged them such that Grace's right hand now lay facedown upon Oliver's palm.

The ring. It was time to give her the ring!

Hands trembling only slightly, he slid the gold band out of his waistcoat pocket. As he slipped it onto her finger, he spoke his favorite lines in the entire ceremony, the ones he'd practiced every night for the past week. These words he knew by heart, because he was speaking them with his soul. He waited until her gaze lifted to his. He wanted her to see that he meant every word.

"With this ring, I thee wed," he said, looking into her eyes. His fingers trembled, but his voice was strong and sure. "With my body, I thee worship. With all my worldly goods, I thee endow. Amen."

Grace's eyes once more blurred behind the sheen of tears, but this time it could not be blamed on unintentional manhandling on the part of Oliver. He could only pray that these were tears of joy, much like those that even now clogged his own throat, rather than tears of sorrow. He would die rather than cause her pain.

The priest lay his hand atop theirs and intoned, "Those whom God hath joined together, let no man put asunder."

Exactly so! Oliver stood even taller, pride mixing unrepentantly with pleasure. His chest puffed a little fuller. She was very nearly his.

"For as much as Grace Halton and Oliver York have consented together in holy wedlock, and have witnessed the same before God and this company, and thereto have given and pledged their troth each to the other, and have declared the same by giving and receiving of a ring, and by joining of hands, I pronounce that they be man and wife together. Amen."

Oliver's knees went weak, and it was all he could do not to swing his bride into his arms and abscond home with her at once. No, not just his bride—his *wife*. Joy swept through him. Only a few more short prayers, and they would be free to go.

"O Lord, save thy servant, and thy handmaid," the priest was droning now.

Oliver's flesh thrummed with excitement. The call-and-response prayer meant they were nearing the end.

"Who put their trust in thee," he responded automatically.

Grace said nothing.

"O Lord," the priest continued, "send them help from thy holy place."

"And evermore defend them..." Oliver's voice trailed off in concern.

Grace still hadn't joined him in speaking the rote lines. In a blinding flash of insight, Oliver belatedly realized why.

His bride didn't know the words. How would she? She hadn't been raised with the Church of England.

Instead, Oliver's deep voice rang out alone as the priest continued his litany. The words echoed in the vast stillness, low and naked without female accompaniment. Oliver swallowed. He tried not to feel as if he alone was pledging eternity here today. His hands still held hers, his ring upon her finger. It didn't matter that she didn't know the words. He would say them for both of them. Just as it didn't signify that she hadn't chosen him. He would love her enough for two. He would love her and honor her and cherish her until she simply cannot help but love him back.

"Almighty God," the priest was saying now.

Oliver gave his bride's hands a fortifying squeeze. This was the final prayer. They'd done it!

"Pour upon you the riches of his grace, sanctify and bless you, that ye may please him both in body and soul, and live together in holy love unto your lives' end. Amen."

Amen.

This time, he did give into temptation. He grabbed up his new wife and swung her in a very small (but still wholly improper) joyous little circle.

Bart and Xavier made their way up front to do their duty as witnesses. Sarah and Ravenwood—two of the most sentimental romantics of Oliver's acquaintance—rushed up to compliment Oliver and Grace on a splendid ceremony. Ravenwood shook Oliver's hand and kissed Grace's cheek. Sarah hugged both of them as best she could with her belly in the way. The moment they finished signing the contract, Bart nudged Sarah out of the way to have their turn shaking Oliver's hand and kissing Grace's cheek.

Oliver never stopped grinning. Not until they stepped outside. Then his joy shattered.

The bride and groom traditionally left together after the ceremony. His carriage was right where he'd left it, with warming bricks and plenty of blankets inside should they need them on their way back home.

But right next to his carriage, the one in which he'd planned to give his new wife her first hundred or so married kisses, was an ominous hired hack. Oliver's head swam, his heart beating much too quickly. *No.* She would not leave him. Not when money could be sent to her mother. He was leaping to conclusions.

His fingers loosened about her hand. "You prefer to follow me home in your own carriage?"

She did not meet his eye. "I have errands I must attend to at once."

At once. Before consummating the marriage. Without even waiting for their guests to disperse. He nodded dumbly. He would not stand in the way of anything that made her happy.

Chapter Seventeen

Grace stared at the dark-haired pawnbroker in horror. "What do you mean, you sold the Black Prince to someone else?"

"Pawnbroking is a business, miss. I got a better price." He lifted a careless shoulder. "End of story."

"A better price than a thousand pounds for a seven hundred pound painting?" she asked in disbelief.

"Two thousand. I'm letting that gift horse keep its teeth."

"Who on earth—"

"Sorry, miss. If there's not something else I can interest you in, I'm going to close up shop for the day. Maybe take the missus on a little holiday."

"Do you mean to say this just happened? Somebody bought it earlier today?"

"About half an hour ago. Can't tell you how glad I am that you were running late. An extra thousand pounds ain't nothing to sniff at."

"I wasn't *late*. I was getting ma—" Grace broke off her explanation and tried to fight the creeping powerlessness weighing down her limbs.

What use was explaining that she'd been at her wedding, which she'd been obligated to complete before coming into possession of the one thousand pounds she did have? Minus the ferry ticket in her reticule. The next boat left at eight o'clock the following morning, and she would be on it. Oliver would be disappointed when she told him, but too many weeks had passed to send a surrogate. She had to see her mother for herself.

She invited the pawnbroker to review the contents of her trunks. The hack she'd hired was still at the berm, the coachman wearily unloading her crates of the gowns. She would sell whatever the pawnbroker would accept, and give as much of her dowry as possible back to Oliver.

Her shoulders slumped. Never had success felt so much like failure.

It was late afternoon by the time she rolled up to Carlisle Manor with what was left of her belongings. She swallowed. Just one night. And then, come what may, she would have to find a way to say good-bye.

As the hired hack crawled to a stop, the great carved doors to the manor house flew open wide.

Oliver burst out onto the stoop. He paused only briefly to shade his eyes from the sun. Upon recognizing the hack as hers, he flew off the front steps and tore across the lawn. She bit her lower lip. He reached the carriage in seconds. Without bothering to allow the driver to dismount, Oliver tossed the coachman a coin and flung open the carriage door to hand her out himself.

Before she could think of anything that might explain her long absence without causing him undue pain, she found herself whisked off the squab and wrapped tight in his arms. If the January wind was still sharp and icy, she could not tell. All she could feel was the solid warmth of his chest, the slight tremble to his powerful arms, his smooth cheek against the top of her head as he held her close.

He pressed a gentle kiss to her temple. "You're back."

"I'm... here." *For tonight*. Lord, was she going to miss him. "I have to go back to America. For my mother. I don't even know if she's alive."

His gaze unfocused. "Let's talk about it tomorrow. I was worried you had already..." He swallowed. "I went to the bank. They said you'd emptied your account. So I came back home." He flashed a wry, embarrassed smile that didn't reach his eyes. Their golden brown depths had dulled, as if no smile would ever reflect there again. "I didn't think you were leaving me, Grace. I thought you were already gone."

Her cheeks flushed. "I did book passage, but I would never leave without telling you. Oliver, I..."

He covered her mouth with his, blocking out her words. Perhaps he knew this was their last night, and hoped he was wrong. Or perhaps, like her, he didn't want to waste what time they had left with the knife of good-bye.

She opened her mouth to him. His tongue was hot, urgent. His kiss was insistent, bruising, but she welcomed it. *Wanted* it. Wished she could give him everything he wanted. She'd wanted him from even before their unplanned tryst in the library. She had wanted him from the moment she'd crashed into his chest and instead of taking her to task, he'd swept her into a waltz.

But she'd always known she couldn't have him, and it was the cruelest twist of irony for Fate to let them marry and still not let her keep him. Her tongue licked against his, tasting him. Memorizing him. The hardness of his chest, his muscles. The softness of his hair as she twisted her fingers in it. The heat of his body despite the cold bite of the wind. The way he held her as if there were nothing more precious to him in this world. And then kissed her with an intensity so carnal it nearly melted the clothes right from her body.

Panting, he lifted his mouth from hers. "I don't care about your money, darling. I only care about *you*."

It was her turn for her smile to fail to meet her eyes. "You get the dowry anyway. Most of it."

He gripped her arms. "What?"

"It should be in your account by now. Mr. Brown promised to complete the transfer within the hour."

"You gave it *back*? Then why did you—"

"I wanted to bring home the Black Prince! I know how much it meant to you. How he felt like family. I took my trunks to the pawnbroker planning to sell every stitch I own to make it happen. But I was too late. Someone had already bought it."

"You…" He gazed at her in wonder, eyes shining as he seemed to replay her words in his mind. When he realized that although she had come back, the Black Prince never would, an edge of pain crept into his eyes. His gaze unfocused, as if his thoughts were now a thousand miles away, chasing after the missing prince. "Is he truly gone?"

She laid her palm against his cheek. "I'm so sorry."

He shook his head. "It doesn't matter. His presence was gone from the moment I took the painting off the wall." His eyes snapped back into focus and narrowed on her face. "Why the devil would you toss away everything you own on that, when there are so many better uses for your money?"

"Because I love you," she blurted. "That painting is the thing you cherish most and I want you to have it!"

"I *have* the thing I cherish most." He swept her off her feet and cradled her to his chest. "You. Right here in my arms. If we weren't standing on my front lawn, right now I'd be loving you with my body as much as I love you with my heart."

Her breath caught as warmth suffused her. She curled her arms about his neck and brushed her lips against his ear. "Then why are we still on the lawn?"

With a dangerous smile, he tightened his grip about her and marched into his house and up to his bedchamber.

All the huge room contained was several square windows, a small table with a pitcher and bowl, and the largest bed Grace had ever laid eyes on. She supposed that was all they really needed. The bed was certainly all she was interested in at the moment.

She squealed with delight as he tossed her right into the middle of the soft mattress and pounced on top of her with a wolfish grin. As she reached up to pull him to her, her stomach fluttered. They were about to make love. If they did this—*when* they did this—they will have consummated their marriage.

Her fingers dug into his hair as her tongue sought his. Her breath came faster. The thought of him pledging his life, his body, to someone else enraged and terrified her. He was *hers*. Every kiss told her so. And yet, she could not guarantee when or if she might return. Everything depended on her mother's health. What if her mother never got well enough for a transatlantic journey? Or what if she did, but it took years to regain enough strength to do so?

Grace wrapped her arms about him tight. She would have to let him go. If she loved him, it was the only choice. But nor could she ignore this passion between them. She could not deny him—or herself—of joining their bodies. Just this once.

For the rest of the day and all night long, she was his.

She tugged at his cravat, yanking it away as quickly as her inexpert fingers could loosen the knots. He sat back on his heels, his hands making quick work of his jacket and waistcoat. His shirtsleeves billowed out along his arms, the fine white linen luminous in the waning sunlight. She stilled his hand when he moved to quit his shirt with the same efficiency. This would be her first view of his bare flesh. She wished to do the honors herself.

With trembling fingers, she ran her hands from his wide shoulders and down his arms. She loved the feel of the cool, slippery linen on the hard muscle of his upper arms. She lifted his hands from his lap and pushed them behind his back. He let them fall to the mattress on either side of her legs.

When she struggled to prop herself up on her elbows, he quickly moved and she knelt before him, knee to knee. Her heart thudded in anticipation.

Slowly, carefully, she tugged the hem of his shirt free from his breeches. His muscles were taut, his skin hot even through the linen, but he remained absolutely motionless as her fingers skimmed the edge of his waistband.

The buckskin of his breeches was buttery soft and molded to the muscles of his thighs. She slid her hands almost to his knees, then back up toward his waistband. This time, her fingers slipped out of sight beneath the hem of his shirt. Instead of the billowy linen, there was only buckskin between her hands and the warm flesh of his thighs.

As her fingers crept higher, the pads of her fingers discovered the wide flaps of his fall, the cloth-covered buttons, the top of his waistband. Her heartbeat doubled as she reached even higher. Her fingers touched his bare skin, his stomach flat and hot and hard. She hooked the hem of his shirt with her thumbs so that her fingers would drag the bottom of his shirt higher as she slid her hands up over his stomach, up over the wide expanse of his chest.

Although it was him she was touching and not the other way around, she sucked in a breath as her fingers learned his body. When her fingertips brushed his nipples, her own tightened painfully beneath her shift. Every bare inch of him seemed to scald her palm.

When she reached his shoulders, he lifted his hands above his head so that she could slide his shirt completely off.

Instead, when the shirt was a cloud of linen about his wrists and forearms, she halted her movement. Imagining she held him captive, she lowered her face to his chest and touched her tongue to his nipple.

He moaned, as if both in pain and pleasure. When she lifted her mouth and pressed her lips to his, his shirt flew across the room. His hands gripped her hips. His mouth devoured hers.

He reached behind her to unlace her gown. She still wore the lavender confection she'd worn to the wedding. She wished she still had the crown of winter jasmine. She would've loved the petals strewn about the bed as she gave herself to her husband completely.

Laces undone, the bodice of her gown gapped open. Echoing her earlier action, he slipped his hands beneath the hem of her skirts and slowly, ever so slowly, began to push it upward.

She was electrified to feel his bare hands on her knees, on her thighs, spreading her legs wider. Her breath came faster. She gasped as cool air licked between her legs, hinting at what was to come. His hands rose higher up her thighs, dragging her skirts up with them. Soon, everything would be bared to the cool air, to the heat of his eyes. An involuntary clench pulsed between her thighs at the thought of herself displayed in that way.

His fingers were now almost to her hips. She held her breath. *Touch me*, she ordered him in her mind. *Touch me touch me touch me.*

He leaned forward, capturing her mouth. His fingers sank between her thighs. The pad of his thumb brushed the upper edge of her thigh, brushed her *there*. His thumb left a trail of wet heat as it stroked her inner thigh. She realized to her surprise that this was *her* heat, *her* wetness upon his fingers. The very realization only made her wetter, hotter, eager for his finger to do it again, to come closer, to press harder.

Without taking her mouth from his, she wiggled her hips a little beneath his hands, hoping he would take the hint without having to express her desire aloud.

Growling, he cupped her exactly where she wanted—and drove one of his fingers inside.

She gasped into his mouth as her body clenched around his finger. It was strange, it was foreign, it was *oh* so sinfully delicious. She wiggled her hips again, not to make him move, but to experiment with the feel of something inside her. Without removing his finger, he brushed his thumb back across the sensitive area he'd touched before. Wet heat coiled within her. Her body gripped him tighter and tighter.

His thumb flicked and circled as a second finger joined the first. Her head fell backward, exposing her neck to him, her bosom. His teeth tugged her loosened bodice from her breast. Her painfully taut nipples sprang up into the cool air.

She couldn't breathe. She couldn't think. There was just his thumb, and his fingers, and now his mouth on her nipple, teasing and suckling just like his thumb was teasing and flicking...

In a burst of pleasure, her body fractured from within, her limbs galvanized as the spasms took her.

When she fell limp and sated against his arm, he lifted the gown over her head, then her shift, her stays. Her body snapped back to awareness. Save for her stockings, she was now naked before him. Her legs widened in invitation. She wanted more. She wanted *him*.

He shucked his boots, his breeches. Despite the fading sunlight, he was beautiful—and very big.

She fell back against the pillows, the sudden frisson of fear unable to dispel the yearning to feel that pleasure again, to experience it together, with him inside her.

He laced his fingers with hers, just above her head, as he positioned his hips over hers. She felt him at her entrance, hot and hard and ready. He slanted his mouth over hers as he began to push inside.

Her fingers squeezed his as her body stretched to fit him. It was pleasure, it was pain. It was perfect. When he was fully sheathed, he lifted his mouth from hers and peppered a line of fervent kisses along the line of her jaw from her chin to her ear.

"Am I hurting you?" he whispered. "I can try to wait a little longer."

"Am I hurting *you*?" she whispered back. When he shook his head, she wrapped her legs about him. "Then if you wait any longer, I will kill you."

Laughing, he squeezed her hands and covered her mouth with his.

Slowly, he began to move. At first gently. Then longer strokes. Faster. Urgent. Demanding. Her body quickened in time with his pace. Her hips rose to meet him, luxuriating in the slide of his body against hers, in the heady fullness of having him inside her at last.

The strokes lengthened, then drove deeper. His kisses never ceased. She recognized the pressure coiling within her. He was going to make her do it again, to squeeze him as he thrust between her legs. He would be able to watch her this time, as the waves took her. He would see the pleasure on her face that he bestowed upon her body. Soon. Very soon. She gripped his hands tight. She wanted him to feel the same!

At the pressure of her fingers, he lifted his mouth from hers. His eyes were ablaze, his face pale, his breath ragged. She thrilled at the passion in his gaze. He *did* feel the same. An intoxicating sense of power flooded her body, and she clenched around him. He gasped and lowered his mouth to the side of her neck. He loosened his grip of her left hand only to tighten his fingers about the slender golden ring he had placed there only a few hours earlier.

"With this ring," he panted against her throat, "I thee wed."

Her thighs clamped tight around him. His thrusts came deeper, more insistent. Making her his.

His mouth brushed the side of her throat. "With my body, I thee worship."

She no longer knew if it was the friction between her legs or the sound of his voice that was driving her over the edge. The pressure was building. Her mind spun even as her hips thrust to meet him. He wasn't just making her his. She was making him hers. Forever.

He dragged his mouth from her throat to her ear and nipped at the lobe. "With all that I have, I thee endow."

She shattered, her hips meeting his as her muscles spasmed around him. He grunted twice and shuddered. Warmth infused her. He lifted his fingers and shoved his hands beneath the pillows as he collapsed on top of her. She slid her arms around his back and hugged him.

He pressed a ragged kiss into her hair. "Wake me up in twelve hours."

She held him tight. How could she possibly leave at dawn? It was impossible.

She could never let him go.

Chapter Eighteen

Grace awoke to the distant sound of carriage wheels grinding across the gravel drive. She yawned. How long had she been asleep? Her hired hack couldn't possibly just now be leaving.

She was tempted to go to the window and find out, but she was also just as tempted to stay right where she was: on her side, her head nestled atop her husband's warm arm, his sleeping body cradling her from behind. She lifted his other hand from her belly to her lips and pressed a kiss to the back of his hand. The pads of his fingers were rough with calluses. She shivered at the memory of their effect upon her nipples, her body.

These were the work-worn hands her grandmother had objected to. Grace threaded her fingers with Oliver's. As far as she was concerned, his fingers wrought nothing but magic.

The rumble of carriage wheels grew closer. Definitely not the hack departing. She slid out of Oliver's grasp. The wedding breakfast! There hadn't been one, so if any of Oliver's friends wished to congratulate them in person, of course they would have to come to the manor to do so. And here they were, naked! At six o'clock in the evening!

She tumbled off the bed in search of her shift, her stays. She was supposed to be a countess now. Which probably meant dressed and presentable when dukes and the like came to call.

"What's happening?" came Oliver's groggy voice from the pillows. "Is it dinner? I could eat an elephant."

Laughing, she tossed his waistcoat in the direction of his head. "It's not the supper gong. I'm afraid we have guests."

"Guests?" Oliver was off the bed and at the window in seconds. He froze at whatever he saw beyond the glass.

Shoulders tight with worry, Grace clutched her gown to her chest and joined him at the window. The distance was still great, but the owners of the stately black carriage were unmistakable. She'd commandeered that very coach just a few weeks earlier.

"My *grandparents* are here?"

He didn't answer. If anything, he seemed excited beyond all cause, his body thrumming with energy. The corners of his mouth twitched. He snatched his breeches up off the floor and began shoving his feet into the legs.

Grace turned back to the window. The tiger had leapt down from his perch and was opening the door. He handed the first person out... Her grandmother, of course. No one would precede her in or out of a carriage. Her grandfather would climb out next, and—

No. The tiger was back, arm high to hand the next person out of the coach. The light was poor and the angle was wrong and the woman stepping out wore a bonnet too big to see her face, but there was no mistaking who had just arrived.

"My *mother*?" she squeaked, her head swimming too dizzily to make much sense out of what she was seeing. "Can this be happening?"

Grace's dress fell from her hands as Oliver hauled her to him and swung her in a circle. "Your mother is finally here."

"You did this?" she gasped, then punched him in the chest. "When? How? Why didn't you tell me?"

"The day I promised to frank your letters. Just as soon as I returned home from the park. I couldn't tell you, not when I didn't know if my mad idea would even bear fruit. I contracted an ex-privateer. I ended up selling the Black Prince to pay for the funds I'd promised him, but—"

"What did you just say?"

"It was my only option. I couldn't waste time sending an emissary on a passenger liner, so I found a pirate for hire. A privateer is a mercenary with a swift ship of his own and not too many questions about the nature of—"

"I know what a privateer is!" she exploded, glaring at him in a mix of awe and fury. "What I cannot believe is that you sold your prized family heirloom in order to hire a pirate to sail to America and kidnap my mother."

Then she laughed. Of course he had done. It was exactly the sort of rescue he would rush out to do.

Unrepentant, Oliver grinned out the window at the front lawn and then back at her. "It worked, didn't it?"

She covered her head with her hands. "You might've told me!"

"I didn't *know* it would work." His expression sobered. "I didn't want to foster hopes if I failed to succeed."

"I was going after her, you ninnyhammer!" She punched his shoulder, then sank back in his arms. He twirled her in laughing, giddy circles. "You did it, Oliver! You saved my mother."

He showered her with kisses. "Now you don't have to go anywhere at all. Except to greet your mother."

He dropped her gown over her head and gave her one last kiss. She shoved her hands through the sleeves and barely waited for him to lace her back up before racing out of his bedchamber and down to the main entrance.

Ferguson held the front door open as she flew outside. The last of her doubts fled from her body. It really *was* her mother. Mama was here!

Grace threw her arms about her mother and held on tight.

"I was so afraid for so long," she whispered into her mother's hair.

Mama held on just as tight. "So was I. When Blackheart showed up—"

Grace stepped back to stare at her mother. "*Who*?"

"The ship's captain. That isn't his given name, of course, but it's difficult to think of a rogue like that as a 'Mister' anything. He's just so..."

Grace's lips quirked. "Piratey, I imagine."

"You wouldn't be wrong. It was quite the adventure. But I was so weak, I slept through most of it."

Grace raised a brow at her husband.

"No, don't blame him. He sent plenty of coin and explicit instructions that I not be moved if I were not able. But of course I came. There isn't much difference between convalescing in my home, and convalescing in a cabin."

"On a pirate ship. In the middle of the ocean. With a man named Blackheart." Grace couldn't believe her ears. "No difference at all."

"I'm just sorry I missed your *wedding*. My fever had just broken, and I was unsteady on my feet—"

"Mama!" Grace's hands reached out to her mother. To be ill, and to make that voyage...

"—so we went to my parents' house." Her brow creased. "Mother got rid of the privateer without so much as a fare-thee-well—"

"As was only right," Grandmother Mayer interrupted with a sniff. "I've never seen such a disreputable blackguard in my life."

"—but then she and Father tucked me abed in front of a warm fire. When next I awoke, we hurried to the church, but we had just missed you and the ceremony was over. My baby! *Married*. I cannot credit it."

Grace put her hand in Oliver's. He kissed the top of her head.

"Mama, it is my deepest pleasure to present to you my husband. Oliver York, Earl of Carlisle." Gooseflesh shivered down Grace's spine as she spoke the words aloud for the first time. Lord Carlisle. Her husband. "Oliver, this is my mother, Mrs. Clara Halton."

He let go of Grace's hand in order to sketch an extremely elegant bow.

Grandmother Mayer rapped Grace's mother in the foot with her walking stick. "See that? *That* is how a gentleman is supposed to greet a lady. Not growling and waving about pistols like a wild animal."

"I collect the pirate made an impression on Grandmother," Grace murmured.

Her mother shook her head, eyes twinkling. "Best we don't talk about that."

"Please. Come inside." Oliver motioned them all toward the house. "I haven't much, but I can at least offer fire to warm you from the cold, and a nice hot cup of tea with milk and honey."

Grandmother nodded and strode toward the manor.

"Just a moment," said Grace's grandfather, nodding his head toward the carriage. "Aren't you forgetting something?"

Mama clasped her hands together. "Oh! Do you mind, Father?"

Before he could so much as open the carriage door, the tiger jumped down from his perch and helped wrest an enormous, paper-wrapped rectangle from inside the coach. An enormous, *princely* sized rectangle.

"I've a different wedding gift for you," Mama said to Grace with a secretive smile. "This one is for your husband."

Oliver's hand shook as he reached out to touch the edge of the brown paper, as if he feared the entirety to be a mirage. At the contact, the paper wrinkled in such a way as to indicate—if it weren't obvious already—that he'd touched the frame of a very large painting.

He stared at Grace's mother in joy and disbelief. "You purchased the Black Prince? For me?"

"*She* didn't." Grandmother jabbed her walking stick in the direction of her husband. "That was Mr. Mayer's doing. Try as I might, he's always been a soft heart. Clara was still asleep. She didn't even know she was rich yet."

Grace blinked at her mother. "You're... rich?"

Mama grinned back at her. "I knew I'd be disowned when I ran away to America. But unbeknownst to me—"

"Or to me," Grandmother interrupted with a harrumph.

"—your grandfather invested my dowry in a trust in my name. It's been collecting an exorbitant amount of interest for twenty-three years. You should *see* the bank statement. I couldn't possibly spend that much in a lifetime." She grasped Grace's hands. "So I'm giving most of it to you. Happy wedding day, daughter."

"To me?" Grace's head swam. More money than could be spent in a lifetime?

"It's mine to give, and I want you to have it. Both of you." Mama arched a brow at Oliver, but her eyes crinkled with humor. "It's my understanding you lovebirds have a bit of refurbishing to do."

Oliver looked as thunderstruck as Grace felt, but he grinned back at her mother. "I believe the first improvement to be made is proper dowager quarters. *Do* say you'll be living with us as part of our family. We dreamed of it even when we hadn't a farthing."

"Well, now you'll have plenty of farthings." Grace's grandmother put in. "Clara is finally home where she belongs, and I credit that miracle wholly to Lord Carlisle. I should have believed you sooner, Grace. If I had, Clara might've arrived weeks ago. Therefore, as our own wedding present to the two of you, Mr. Mayer and I will be matching the sum your mother gives." She narrowed her steely eyes at Oliver. "But don't go offering me dowager quarters. I still prefer my own home, thank you very much."

"Matching..." Grace could barely even choke out the words. "But grandmother, you don't even *like* Oliver!"

"Perhaps not at first. But he helped me get Clara back. That alone is worth any price." She cast Oliver a speculative glance. "Although, I'll admit I knew there was more to him than met the eye when I saw his bare hands. Your grandfather had calluses just like that for many, many years. They may not be the hands of an earl, but they're the hands of a *man*."

Grace's mouth fell open, but not a single sound came out.

"Now then." Grandmother rapped Oliver on the shoulder with her walking stick and turned toward the manor. "How about that cup of tea?"

The End

Thank You For Reading

I hope you enjoyed this story!

Sign up at EricaRidley.com/club99
for members-only freebies
and new releases for 99 cents!

Reviews help other readers like you.

Reviews help readers find books that are right for them.
Please consider leaving a review wherever you purchased
this book, or on your favorite review site.

Let's be friends! Find Erica on:

www.EricaRidley.com
facebook.com/EricaRidley
twitter.com/EricaRidley
pinterest.com/Erica_Ridley

Join the Dukes of War facebook group for giveaways and
exclusive content:
http://facebook.com/groups/DukesOfWar

**Did you know there are more
books in this series?**

This romance is part of
the Dukes of War
regency-set historical series.

In order, the Dukes of War books are:

The Viscount's Christmas Temptation
The Earl's Defiant Wallflower
The Captain's Bluestocking Mistress
The Major's Faux Fiancée
The Brigadier's Runaway Bride
The Duke's Accidental Wife

**Other Romance Novels
by Erica Ridley:**

Too Wicked To Kiss (2010)
Too Sinful To Deny (2011)
Let It Snow (2013)
Dark Surrender (2014)

About the Author

Erica Ridley learned to read when she was three, which was about the same time she decided to be an author when she grew up.

Now, she's a *USA Today* bestselling author of historical romance novels. Her latest series, The Dukes of War, features roguish peers and dashing war heroes who return from battle only to be thrust into the splendor and madness of Regency England.

When not reading or writing romances, Erica can be found riding camels in Africa, zip-lining through rainforests in Central America, or getting hopelessly lost in the middle of Budapest.

For more information, please visit EricaRidley.com.

Acknowledgments

As always, I could not have written this book without the invaluable support of my critique partners. Huge thanks go out to Janice Goodfellow, Emma Locke, Darcy Burke, and Erica Monroe for their advice and encouragement. You are the best!

I also want to thank the amazing Dukes of War facebook group. Your enthusiasm makes the romance happen. Thank you so much!

Next in the series:

The
Captain's
Bluestocking
Mistress

The Captain's Bluestocking Mistress

Captain Xavier Grey's body is back amongst the *beau monde*, but his mind cannot break free from the horrors of war. His friends try to help him find peace. He knows he doesn't deserve it. Just like he doesn't deserve the attentions of the sultry bluestocking intent on seducing him into bed...

Spinster Jane Downing wants off the shelf and into the arms of a hot-blooded man. Specifically, the dark and dangerous Captain Grey. She may not be destined to be his wife, but nothing will stop her from being his mistress. She could quote classical Greek by the age of four. How hard can it be to learn the language of love?

CPSIA information can be obtained
at www.ICGtesting.com
Printed in the USA
LVHW02s0758280518
578666LV00002B/490/P